College for Sinners

LAWRENCE BLOCK
writing as Andrew Shaw

COLLEGE FOR SINNERS

LAWRENCE BLOCK writing as ANDREW SHAW

Copyright © 1960 Lawrence Block

All Rights Reserved.

Cover and Interior Design by QA Productions

A LAWRENCE BLOCK PRODUCTION

CLASSIC EROTICA

---

21 Gay Street
Candy
Gigolo Johnny Wells
April North
Carla
A Strange Kind of Love
Campus Tramp
Community of Women
Born to be Bad
College for Sinners
Of Shame and Joy
A Woman Must Love
The Adulterers
The Twisted Ones
High School Sex Club
I Sell Love
69 Barrow Street
Four Lives at the Crossroads
Circle of Sinners
A Girl Called Honey
Sin Hellcat
So Willing

Classic Erotica #10

College for Sinners

Lawrence Block

CHAPTER 1

Many years ago, when the college was young and the city not much older, the college stood in the wilderness. Both the city and the college were on an island. The city was located at the southern tip of the island and the college was far to the north. With the passage of time, the city had grown and the college had remained where it was, until finally it was surrounded by smoke and steel, brick and wood.

The college was located at Broadway and 116th Street in New York City. To the east and to the north Harlem stretched out far and wide, a wilderness of black and brown and white. To the west was the Hudson River, to the south, the middle of Manhattan.

It was early autumn and the college was beginning to stir itself from the pleasant monotony of summer vacation and to shift into gear for the year ahead. The campus was alive once again with students—boys with crew-cut hair and horn-rimmed glasses, boys with tweed jackets and khaki slacks, boys with books under their arms and briefcases in their hands. It was a co-educational college, and the boys were not alone. There were also girls in sweaters and skirts, girls in blouses and slacks, girls with pony tails and Italian haircuts and free-swinging, shoulder-length hair. There were brunettes and redheads and blondes, big-breasted girls and flat-chested girls, tall girls and short girls, thin girls and fat girls.

There was a bright-eyed blonde who measured 36-24-36 and there was a dull-eyed brunette who measured 24-36-45.

There were professors and associate professors and assistant professors and instructors who ranged in age from twenty-five to seventy-six. There was a peanut vendor who had made a poor but honest living for twenty-five years selling peanuts to the students and faculty of the college, and there was a bookmaker who had made a good but dishonest living for ten years taking bets from the students and faculty of the college. God was in his heaven and all was well with the world.

The boy was sitting in the room at a desk. The room was a cubicle hardly large enough for one person; amazingly enough, it was designed to hold two persons, with a bed for each and a desk for each and a dresser for each. The desks were small, ugly, and the last word in functional modern design. The beds, stacked one on top of the other, and the dressers, similarly stacked one on top of the other, took up as little room as possible. The one closet was filled with clothing which had been certified to be *de rigueur* for campus wear, the proper uniform for the scholastic soldier.

The boy at the desk was in uniform. On his feet he wore argyle socks and white buckskin shoes. His pants were khaki, his shirt white oxford cloth with a button-down collar. The shirt was open at the neck and the sleeves were rolled up.

The boy was tall, a little on the thin side. His hair was very light blonde, almost white, and cut very short. His eyes were blue. He was nineteen years old and he looked a year or two younger. His name was David Forrester.

He was a sophomore at the college, a Boston boy majoring in biology with three years to go before he would have a B.A. in his pocket. Then four more years of graduate work, give or take a year depending upon where he went and what he did, and he'd be ready either to grab off a good industrial job or settle down as a member of the academic profession, making the slow trip from instructor to assistant to associate to professor.

Right now he wasn't sure which he wanted—a well-paying job or a teaching slot. The two both appealed from time to time. The job meant money, position. The academic berth meant security, time for research, the feeling that he was accomplishing something instead of selling out. But he had years to make up his mind. He didn't have to decide right away. In the meantime he had enough to worry about, the first and foremost worry being the schedule of courses for the year.

He stared hard at the sheet of paper in front of him and tried his damnedest to concentrate on it. The light was poor—a goose-neck desk lamp did what it could to help out, but didn't accomplish a hell of a lot. Dave Forrester's mind raced, trying to concern itself with Invertebrate Biology and Organic Chemistry and 101s and 202s and credit hours and professors.

And failed miserably.

Because, at the moment, Dave Forrester couldn't have cared less about Invertebrate Biology and Organic Chemistry and 101s and 202s and credit hours and professors. Dave Forrester, as a matter of fact, could not have given less of a damn about the whole academic routine. What he cared about had to do with his academic specialty, admittedly. He specialized in biology, and no one in his right mind would deny that Dave's interest was biological. Biological as all hell, as a matter of fact.

He wanted a woman.

He took a cigarette from a pack and put it between his lips, then lit it with the lighter his folks had given him a year ago when he had trundled off to college filled with high hopes and earnest expectations. He dragged on the cigarette and inhaled deeply, wondering what the smoke was doing to the tissues of his lungs. He didn't particularly care.

That he wanted a woman was not remarkable. The average man spends every minute of his life either wanting a woman or having one. What *was* somewhat remarkable was the fact that Dave Forrester, nineteen-year-old sophomore at the college, had never *had* a woman.

First there was high school. While other red-blooded lads were lifting red-blooded girls' skirts in the schoolyard (and, occasionally, leaving a little blood on the gravel as a grim souvenir) Dave Forrester was busy getting top grades, delivering prescriptions for a neighborhood druggist, and otherwise amusing himself in a generally asexual manner.

Then there was college. And, since he had not known a girl in New York outside of the coeds, and since the coeds were all getting a hot and heavy rush from the upperclassmen, Dave Forrester, like most of his classmates, had had a hot total of three dates in the course of the year. They had been an enjoyable trio of dates, and he had kissed each of the three girls once or twice, but that had been the end of it.

Then there was the summer.

The idea of spending the summer in Boston with good old

Mom and good old Dad, had been revolting, to say the least. The idea of spending the summer as a nature counselor in an expensive camp in Maine had made a good deal more sense to him, and that was where he had wound up. The work was not too difficult—since he was a specialty counselor, he was relieved of the chore of having a cabin full of urchins to look after—and nature counseling was close enough to his own interests to keep him from dying of boredom. But speaking truthfully one would have to admit that the high point of the summer was a girl named Sheila Reeves.

They had hit it off right away, he and Sheila. She was a year younger than he was, a pretty little brunette with a good body who was killing a summer before running off to her first year at Michigan State. She had liked him, and he had liked her, and things came to a head rather quickly.

He killed the cigarette and sat back in the uncomfortable desk chair and remembered . . .

It was late at night. The campers were in bed. They were also asleep, hopefully, although the little bastards demonstrated an astounding facility for staying awake far into the night. Now, however, both Dave and Sheila were acting on the assumption that their charges were snug in Dreamland.

They were down by the lake.

Every respectable camp has a lake, and the lake serves two functions. During the day, the kids swim in it. At night, counselors sit by it in pairs and pretend that they are in love. Which, more or less, was what Dave and Sheila were doing.

He put his arm around her and drew her close. Her eyes were dancing and her face was slightly flushed.

He kissed her.

It started out like any old kiss and picked up speed as it moved along. It moved quite a distance. Her arms went around him and held him, and he could feel the warm softness of her breasts pressed tight against his chest. Her lips opened and his tongue snuck between them, caressing the inside of her lips, slipping between her teeth and probing the warm sweetness of her hungry mouth.

Her tongue met his and they touched, stroked. A little gasp tore from somewhere deep within the confines of her throat.

Then she was pushing him away.

"Sheila—"

"Let's . . . relax, Dave." She spoke with difficulty, her eyes closed and her hands clenched into tight fists.

"Sheila—"

"We don't want to get too involved," she said. "We don't want to start something that we can't finish. Let's . . . just talk, sort of. Tell me how your day went. Tell me what's new in the Nature Hut. Things like that."

"To hell with the Nature Hut."

"Dave—"

He reached for her and she did not stop him. He felt very confident, very sure of himself and he took her in his arms and lowered her down upon the cool moist grass. He lay next to her and their bodies touched from their knees to their shoulders. The contact was very exciting.

They kissed again and it was even better than the first time.

This time her tongue was the aggressor, the hunter, and his mouth was more than willing to receive her. While they kissed his hands ran over her soft wool sweater. He couldn't see the color in the dark but he remembered that it was yellow. The sight of her breasts pushing the front of that yellow sweater out of shape was a very vivid picture in his mind.

Now he had her rolled over on her back and his hand moved very gently over the front of the sweater. He touched her breast, then moved his hand away, then touched her again.

Her voice was dreamy. "That feels so nice," she said. "It can't be wrong, can it? Not when it feels this good. Keep touching me like that. I love it."

He kissed her once more and each of his hands found a breast to hold onto. His hands were bolder now and they squeezed the full firm flesh of her breasts in a magnificent rhythm, tensing, relaxing, tensing, relaxing. He felt her nipples stiffen under his hands and he knew that she wanted him just as he wanted her, that she needed him as he needed her.

Maybe this would be the night. There was only one more week before camp ended for the summer, one more week before he went back to Boston and she went back to wherever the hell she lived and they forgot each other forever. Just one more week to get to her, one more week to make her virginity a thing of the past. One week wasn't much time.

"Dave—"

He stopped her mouth with a kiss and tugged at her sweater, trying to pull it loose from beneath her skirt. He managed to get his hands under her sweater and run them up her belly to her breasts. She was wearing a bra, but his hands discovered how little need she had for it.

Her breasts were firm and very big. Once before he had put his hands under her sweater and touched her like this. Now, however, it was not enough.

He wanted more.

"Sit up," he said.

"But—"

"Sit up."

She sat up, looked lost and slightly apprehensive as he pulled the woolly yellow sweater over her head. He tossed it onto the grass and stared at her, his eyes warm.

"I'm worried," she said. "Dave, suppose somebody comes and sees us like this."

"So what?"

"I'm afraid," she said. She held up her hands, trying to cover herself. He wondered whether she was afraid of being discovered or afraid of what they were going to do. It was hard to tell—she simply seemed to be afraid in general, and he knew the best way to assuage her fear was to ignore it.

"Dave—"

"Shut up," he said. He reached for her again and tumbled her down upon the grass, his mouth finding hers once more, his hands on her body. He squeezed her breasts harder than before and began to talk to her.

"You're not afraid," he said. "You love it."

She moaned softly.

"You like it when I touch you like this," he said. "I know you do. Tell me how much you like it."

She moaned a little more deeply and he reached around her, his fingers searching for the clasp of the brassiere. He had a little trouble with it but then all at once the bra was open and he pulled it away from her. Her breasts were free now and he could only stare at them, too awed by the sight to do a thing.

The rest of her body was tanned from the sun. But her breasts were two creamy white mounds of firm flesh lightly crisscrossed with ice blue veins. Her nipples were pink roses, saucy peaks for the two perfect hills of womanliness.

"Do you like them?"

"They're beautiful."

"Then touch them."

He touched her, marveling that anything in the world could be so sweet and soft. Now, with her bare breasts in his hands for the first time, he realized just how big they were. They were very big, and very nice.

She groaned with passion.

"I don't care if anybody comes," she said. "I don't care what happens. I just want you to touch me like that. Nothing ever made me feel this way before, Dave. Nothing in the world ever felt this good. This is so nice it's driving me out of my mind. It . . . it feels so good!"

He kept touching her and he knew that he had to have her or go mad, that if they stopped short of fulfillment he would not be able to control himself.

"Play with the nipples," she said. "Touch them. Oh, that's good. They're so sensitive. You have no idea how sensitive they are. It drives me wild when you touch them."

Suddenly he bent down and pressed his mouth to her breast.

He kissed her with his lips together at first, then opened them and let his tongue trail gently over the soft skin.

The effect was startling.

She began to writhe beneath him, her whole body churning almost spasmodically. Her hands reached for him. One stroked the back of his neck and the other pressed down on the back of his head, holding his mouth against her breast.

"Kiss it," she said. "Kiss the nipple. Kiss it! Do everything to it."

His lips moved around her stiff nipple in ever-diminishing concentric circles. He was teasing her now, toying with her passion, raising her higher and higher.

"Kiss it!" she cried. "Please!"

He kissed hard on the nipple and felt her turn into a creature of pure passion. His other hand held her other breast and his fingers closed on the nipple. Everything he did only served to heighten their mutual excitement.

Then his hand, the hand that was not on her breast, dropped to the hem of her skirt. He felt her go stiff from head to foot. She knew what was coming next but she wasn't doing anything about it.

Slowly, gradually, his hand snuck beneath the hem of the skirt. He touched her leg below her knee, and all the while his mouth and his fingers were busy with her breasts. He could sense the two forces at battle within her lovely body, one responding to the thrills of what he was doing to her, the other struggling to control her desires, fighting to keep her from giving in to him.

"Dave ... Dave, please don't ... don't do anything we shouldn't. Dave ... don't—"

His hand reached her knee and squeezed it gingerly. The hand moved up onto her thigh. Her thighs were clutched tight together but the hand pushed between them, searching, reaching, hungry for her.

Then he touched her.

She stiffened.

"Stop," she said. "Please, Dave, I don't want to. I won't do it, honest to God I won't, I don't want to."

He wanted to slap the daylights out of her. His own excitement was even greater than hers and he couldn't take any more teasing, any more waiting. But he knew he had to play his cards right. She was a virgin, and she wouldn't let him make love to her unless he simply got her so excited that she couldn't help herself.

So he found himself saying: "Don't worry, Sheila. Darling, don't worry. We won't do anything you don't want to do. I promise you that, honey."

She seemed to relax and he pushed on.

"I just want to touch you," he said. "I just want to make you feel good. I wouldn't try to . . . to do anything. I just want to touch you because I know you like it."

She didn't say anything and his hand moved upward beneath her skirt, right back to where it had been.

"You like this, don't you?"

No answer. He touched her some more and received tangible evidence that she liked it.

"How does it feel?"

"Wonderful!" The word was a gasp.

"And this?"

"God!"

"And this?"

Her answer was a low and desperate moan.

Then: "Dave, you meant it, didn't you?"

"Huh?"

"About . . . not going all the way. Because . . . well, I always thought it was bad for boys if they got very excited and didn't go all the way."

"It's all right," he lied.

"Because," she went on, "I . . . like it when you touch me. You know how much I like it. And if you promise not to try to go all the way I'll let you do everything you want. But maybe you won't want to. If it's painful, or anything."

"I promise."

"Are you sure?"

"I'm sure."

She giggled. "It's supposed to be the girl who has to control the boy," she said. "But it isn't working that way. I mean, when you touch me like that I just lose all control. I get so excited I can't see or think or anything. When you keep touching me like that it gets me wild."

That was comforting.

"But you said you could stop," she went on. "I don't know if I could make you stop, but I . . . I trust you. You can do whatever you want, but you have to stop before anything . . . well, happens. You know what I mean."

He knew what she meant.

"You'll be careful, won't you?"

"Of course," he said.

"Because otherwise I don't know what would happen."

But I do, he thought savagely. *You'll get laid. That's exactly what will happen.*

"Touch me some more," she said. "And kiss me. Do everything to me."

Now, because he had made the silly promise that he fully intended to break along with her maidenhead, he didn't have to play games any more. He made her lie flat on her back with her eyes closed while he removed her skirt and her socks and shoes. Then, except for her panties, she was absolutely naked. He let his eyes run over her body from head to toe, studying every magnificent detail of her.

Then his hands followed his eyes. He touched her flat stomach and her soft shoulders. He touched her breasts and her nipples and felt desire return to them as they went stiff and firm. He kissed them and she moaned in his ears.

His hands dropped lower, gripping her thighs. He began to touch her again, touching her where he knew she very literally ached to be touched, and her body churned rhythmically, flawlessly.

Then his fingers hooked under the elastic waistband of the flimsy white panties and drew them over her hips. She was helping him now, arching her back so that he could get the panties over her hips and down and off.

He removed them, dropped them on the grass, and looked at the very essence of her.

"God," she moaned. "Nothing ever made me feel like this before, Dave. Nothing in the world. I didn't know anything could be so good. I didn't know anything could get me so excited. When you touch me like that it drives me wild. It drives me out of my mind, Dave. I . . . I go wild. I can't lie still. I have to squirm all over the place and I can't lie still."

She suited her actions to her words, moving her hips as he kissed her.

"Take off your clothes," she said. "Take off your clothes, Dave."

Be pulled his tee-shirt over his head, touching her with one hand while he did so. He couldn't let her cool off, not now, not when he was inches away from success. He had to keep her eager, keep her boiling over.

And then they would get down to business.

"I want you naked," she was saying. "I want you naked with your clothes off and I want to see you and touch you. Hurry up, Dave. Please hurry!"

He was so excited himself that he wanted to scream his head off.

"Dave—"

Her hands were very soft on him. She touched him and he knew that he had to have her, that if he had ever entertained the thought of stopping short of his goal that thought was now gone forever.

She touched him, squeezed him. Her whole body went rigid as wrought iron for the shadow of a second—then she was a tigress again, flat on her back with her arms out and her breasts pointing like sentinels at the sky. Her knees were bent and her parted thighs offered Heaven to him.

"Do it," she begged. "Do it to me. Forget what I said before. Forget everything. Please do it. Do it to me, I love you, I need it, to hell with your promise."

He reached for her.

"The promise doesn't matter," she said. "I don't care about it, I changed my mind, it's my right to change my mind. I just need you and it's so good and I need it so much—"

And then, three short inches from Heaven, it happened.

He didn't understand it at first. Then he realized just what had taken place. They had spent far too much time on the preliminaries, and he had grown far too excited, and that was a mistake.

A bad mistake.

A fatal mistake.

An unforgivable mistake.

Too much excitement. Too much kissing and caressing.

Too much excitement when her hands had reached for him and touched him and caressed him.

Too much.

And too soon.

Because, just when it was time for the main event to begin, just when she was more than ready and more than willing, the ball game was very definitely over. He reached the peak way ahead of schedule, and while she moaned and thrashed in his arms he lay upon her limp and spent and out of the running.

It took a long while before he managed to explain to her just what had happened and just what, therefore, would *not* happen that night. Explaining was not easy. He was worried that she would blame him, that she would hate him.

He was not sure, for that matter, whether she would hate him more for trying or for failing. But he was certain that, one way or the other, she would hate him. She would hate him for breaking his promise, and she would hate him for not being enough of a man to break his promise with a bang. For one reason or for another, or for both, she would hate him.

That's what he thought.

But he was wrong.

Dead wrong.

Because, as it turned out, she thought he was the greatest thing since canned beer. She thought he had been struggling manfully to avoid breaking his promise, and she thought it was all her fault for holding out to begin with, and the upshot of it all was that she was all in favor of him, and all in favor of love, and that everything was coming up roses.

"You're sweet," she said, "and I've been silly. What we almost did wasn't bad. For goodness sake, we both enjoyed it and nobody got hurt or anything and—"

She broke off suddenly, as if she realized all at once that she was naked and that he was naked and that she certainly ought to be embarrassed. But, happily enough, she was not embarrassed at all. Shyly she reached out a hand and touched him.

"Poor little man," she said. "Humble now."

"Uh-huh."

"Your ego is deflated," she went on. "That's a good name for it, wouldn't you say?"

He laughed in spite of himself.

"Everything's going to be good now," she said. "We've got four days before camp ends. Four days is a pretty short time but it's going to be enough."

"Enough for what?"

"Enough for us, silly. Enough for you to make a woman out of me. Enough for us to set a few records. Oh, God, I'm talking like

a tramp. But you know what? I think I like talking like a tramp.
Do I sound horrible?"

"Nope. Sort of nice."

"Not even wicked?"

"A little wicked."

"That's good," she said. "I think I like sounding wicked. And
I think I'm going to like *being* wicked. God, I was silly. Asking
you to hold back. I'm not going to ask that tomorrow. Or the day
after. Or the day after that or the day after that. I'm going to be the
wickedest girl in the world."

They got dressed very slowly, looking at each other from time
to time, and then they kissed each other several times. The kisses were intense without being passionate, and he knew that they
were, more than anything else, promises of things to come.

He walked her back to her cabin. Then he took her in his arms
and kissed her again.

"Dave—"

He held her close.

"I'm sorry about tonight."

"Why?"

"Because of what happened. I mean of what didn't happen. I
was afraid."

"You were a woman," he said. "Maybe that amounts to the
same thing. But don't talk like that. Tonight was sort of fun,
wasn't it?"

She grinned.

"See?"

"Tomorrow," she said firmly. "Tomorrow I am going to become a woman. You'll have to be gentle with me, Dave. I . . .

haven't done it before, you know, and I may not know what to do. You'll have to show me."

He wondered vaguely who was going to show him.

"Have you . . . had many girls?"

"Not too many," he said, almost honestly.

"Were they very pretty?"

"Not as pretty as you."

"Did you love them?"

"No."

The next question, he knew, was going to be something along the lines of *Do you love me?* and that was the sort of question he wanted to avoid. So he kissed her again and she stopped talking. Then, just before he turned and left her there, she took his hand and clasped it between her thighs.

It was another promise.

That night and the next day he wondered just how he had managed to step in offal and come up smelling of ambergris. All he knew was that he had been trying his damnedest to seduce her, had won the battle and lost the war, and now he was on top of the world through no fault of his own. Actually, it had worked out even better than if they had made love.

If he had managed to seduce her, then she would have been an unwilling participant at best. Her passion might have carried her far enough so that they would have been able to complete the act without much discomfort, but afterward she would have been pretty teed off about the whole thing.

She would have blamed him for breaking the promise, and she would have loathed him, and there would have been no repeat performance. As things stood, there were four wonderful days to look forward to. The affair would last the season, then break quickly with no loose ends. He would be a man when he got back to school.

He dreamed about her that night, and when he awoke he had three-dimensional evidence that she was still on his mind. He took a cold shower and went out to breakfast.

The day dragged.

The day ended.

The night arrived.

And he saw her.

And the bomb fell.

During the night and during the day he had known in some hidden corner of his mind that something simply had to come along and foul things up. This was just moving along too perfectly for him, and something had to serve as the wooden shoe in the machinery, the stumbling block to happiness, the joker in the deck, the spade in the woodpile.

He had tried to dismiss the thought, but it was a persistent one.

And, as it turned out, it was a correct one.

He met her by the lake. He was ready and willing and able, but there was a very strange light in her eyes. He thought that maybe she had changed her mind, that the girl who had wanted to be wicked had enlisted on the side of the angels. He wasn't too worried, though. She was a passionate girl, and a few caresses would be sure to put her in the proper mood.

"Dave," she said, "I don't know how to tell you this."

"Tell me what?"

"I . . . don't know how to say it."

"Go on."

"Well . . . I'm not pregnant."

"I should hope not," he said. "We haven't done anything yet, have we?"

"You don't understand."

"You're right."

"The reason I know I'm not pregnant," she went on, "is that I'm having my period."

His heart sank.

"And you know what that means."

He knew what that meant.

"Sheila," he said very slowly, "when you have your . . . period . . . how long does it last?"

"Four days."

"Four . . . days?"

"Or five," she said sadly. "Never any less than that."

"Oh," he said. "Well, I guess I'll see you next year."

CHAPTER 2

With an angry shake of his head he capped his fountain pen and pushed the papers out of the way on his desk. Then, giving up completely, he switched off the desk lamp and walked over to the bed. The top bunk was his—Bill Jergens, his roommate, had the lower—and he hauled himself up on top of it and stretched out.

It was no use. Remembering the passionate merry-go-round with Sheila had only made things just so much worse. He couldn't get any work done, not with his brain filled to overflowing with breasts and hips and thighs.

He needed a woman.

The obvious course of action was to go out and buy a woman. But, like almost everybody, he had firmly decided once long ago that his first love would not be one he had to pay for. It seemed at the time like an intelligent and noble decision. Now it seemed more than a little ridiculous.

What the hell, he thought. It wasn't as though he had time to sit around and wait for a vision of loveliness to float into his arms. If he sat around waiting, he was not going to accomplish a hell of a lot. He'd spend the whole year dreaming about sex. And, as a biology major, he knew damned well that this was biologically unsound.

He needed a woman.

Breathing deeply, he rolled over on his side, squinted, and looked at the clock on his dresser. According to the clock it was now twenty minutes after eleven. A rapid check of the contents of his wallet indicated that he had approximately twenty-three dollars in cash, plus whatever change was on his desk.

He could afford a maximum of fifteen dollars. Now all he had to do was find a whore.

He swung himself out of the bed, slipped on the shoes he had kicked off, and left the room. A poker game was in progress in the hall and he turned down an invitation to take a hand. He had better things to do.

He went downstairs, left the dormitory, reached the street. The weather was autumn in New York—not too warm, not too cold, with a sliver of moon in the sky.

Where next?

He was baffled. There had to be some specific place where whores were picked up, but he had no idea where it might be. And he couldn't think of anybody to ask. He wandered rather blindly along Broadway, waiting for something to happen, and something happened.

"Hi, Dave! You *are* Dave, aren't you?"

He looked down and saw a very beautiful little blonde, a short girl with a perfect figure and very light blue eyes. It seemed out of the question that this girl could remember him and that he could not recollect ever seeing her before.

"I'm Dave, all right," he admitted. "But—"

"But you don't know who I am?"

"That's about the size of it."

"That figures," she said. "We never met."

"But—"

"I was behind you in registration line," she admitted, "and I peeked over your shoulder when you were filling out one of those foolish cards, and I saw your name. And now I recognized you, and I thought I'd say hello, and I already said hello before I remembered that we never met. It's very confusing, you see. This is just my second day here and I've met so many people and I can't keep my head on straight, if you know what I mean, and—"

"What's your name?"

"Jan."

"Just Jan? No last name?"

"Jan Chatterton. They call me Chatterbox for short. If you want to be nice now, you'll tell me that you can't imagine why they call me that. But I guess the age of chivalry is dead as a lox. I also guess I talk too much. Don't you think so?"

"Well—"

"You're sweet," she said, "and it's a nice night out, and if you ask me to go for a cup of coffee with you I will almost undoubtedly accept."

He looked at her. Looking at the perfection of her body just made him want her that much more. And, while going for a walk with her certainly had a great deal of appeal, he very definitely had better things to do. A walk with Jan Chatterton might be fun and all that, but it would not accomplish the important feat of making his loss of virginity a *fait accompli*.

And if there was one *fait* that he wanted to *accompli*, it was just that.

"Look," he said, "it's a fine notion, and I'd like to but I can't. Not tonight."

Her face fell.

"Tomorrow," he went on, "would be another story. Are you free tomorrow?"

She shook her head.

"You're not?"

"Of course not," she said. "I have a date with a boy named Dave Forrester. Pick me up around eight or so, will you? I'm living in Kallett Hall. If you forget my name just ask them for the noisy little one. They'll know who you mean. I've got quite a following already, you see. Everybody knows and loves me. Everybody listens to me. They have no choice. I don't let them get a word in edgewise. I'll see you at eight, Dave. Bye."

And, incredibly, she was gone.

He shook a cigarette out of his pack, lit it, then crossed Broadway and walked into the first bar he saw. He ordered a beer and nursed it along, trying to figure out what to do next. Maybe a cab, he thought. Cabbies knew all about things like that. He could just hop in a cab and tell the driver to take him to a good house. That might work.

Then again, it might not. The cabby might get mad at him or something. Or the cabby might turn out to be a cop, or might not know where a house was, or . . .

He turned around when his shoulder was tapped.

"Good evening, David, my boy. You look down, son. Very far down. Problems?"

The boy who spoke was a senior named Keith Talbot. They had met the year before, when Dave was a freshman and Talbot a junior. Dave had sort of liked and disliked Talbot in about equal measure. The guy was certainly very sharp—a campus intellectual, a respected near-alcoholic, a big man with the girls. But there had always been something about Talbot that made him a little bit nervous.

Talbot was tall and broad-shouldered. His hair was jet black and neatly combed. He was a bundle of affectations, from the Sherlock Holmes pipe he smoked to the black goatee on his chin. He dressed very well, never without a jacket and tie, but there was a quality of purposeful sloppiness to him notwithstanding.

But today something about Talbot inspired confidence. If anybody knew where the whores were hiding, Talbot would know. And Talbot would help him out.

"Problems," he admitted. "Can I buy you a beer?"

"Why not go all out and buy me a shot to go with it?" Grinning, Keith Talbot sat down next to Dave and waved a finger at the bartender. The stout man hurried over, poured a double shot of bourbon and drew a beer for a chaser. Talbot drank the shot down in one swallow and sipped the beer.

"Tell Uncle Keith."

He shifted uncomfortably. "It's like this," he said. "I need a woman."

"Who doesn't?"

"A whore," Dave said. "A prostitute."

"And you're broke? You want to borrow the price?"

"I've got the money."

"Then what's the problem?"

"I don't know where to find one."

Talbot threw back his head and roared. "I'll be dipped in it," he said. "Well, my boy, you came to the right place."

"Here?"

"No, not the bar, damn it. Me! Davey, if I can't find you a woman, then there aren't any left in New York. And if there aren't any left in New York, then the population of this town has fallen pretty drastically. Your problem is solved as of this minute, Dave. Old Uncle Keith will take care of everything."

Dave felt better at once. But, at the same time, he was a little bit nervous. There was some quality in Keith that he could not quite pin down. Whatever it was, it certainly didn't inspire confidence. Keith had the type of personality that kept you on edge ninety percent of the time.

"How much can you spend, Dave?"

"Fifteen dollars. Less, if it's possible."

"Hmmmm. You mind dark ones?"

He looked blank.

"Negro girls," Keith translated. "We're just a few blocks from Harlem. And I know a good place up there. The girls are clean and the price is right. Unless you have something against colored girls, of course. Some people do. Frankly, I've never been able to tell the difference."

"It's all the same to me."

"Fine," Talbot said. "Let's go."

"Are you . . . coming along?"

"Of course," Keith said. "A trick a day keeps the doctor away, you know."

They left the bar and walked north on Broadway. Dave suggested taking a cab but Talbot vetoed the idea, explaining that it was just a short walk and that the air wouldn't hurt them. Besides, he said, it wouldn't hurt to get there a little later on. After midnight on a week night the girls didn't get as much business.

The prices went down and the girls didn't rush through each performance.

"Where is the house?"

"It's not a house exactly," Keith said.

"It isn't?"

"More of an area. The corner of Saint Nicholas and 126th Street is the place. The girls wander around on the street there. You pick them up and they take you to a hotel right on the corner. Two bucks for the hotel and whatever you and the girl agree on. It shouldn't run more than ten all told."

"And it's safe?"

"Perfectly safe," Keith said. "Hell, the girls who walk around up there are the same ones who hustle downtown on Seventh Avenue. They're the same ones the Times Square pimps tout you to. The only difference is that they're right next to the hotel. No cab fare, no middlemen. That keeps the cost down."

They continued north on Broadway to 125th Street, then headed east toward Saint Nicholas Avenue. On the way Dave was glad that Keith was with him. It wasn't as though he was afraid to walk by himself. But he felt a little panicky, knowing that in a very short time he was going to make love to a woman for the first time in his life. And it helped to have somebody along to talk to him.

"Whores are funny," Keith was saying. "Far as I'm concerned, they can't compare to a girl who wants to go on her own accord. You get a girl who's hungry and no whore can compare to her. Not only that, but there's that good feeling you get from making a girl all on your own without having to pay for the privilege. Hell, you know what I mean."

Dave agreed solemnly.

"But whores sure come in handy," Keith went on. "Say you want something a little more complex. Something a little bit out of the ordinary. It takes a hell of a lot of work before you can get a regular girl to do it. With a whore all you need is the price. Some tricks cost more than other tricks, but you get what you pay for."

"Sure," Dave said. Personally, he didn't care what sort of specialties the whores were ready and able to provide. He just wanted a woman, and it didn't matter how he had her.

But Keith breezed on. "One girl I knew," he said. "A whore, all right. But the thing to do was to go find her around ten in the morning. Imagine going to one at ten in the morning! But with her it was worth it. You see, she'd wake up eager as all hell first thing in the morning. And the guy who got there first really had something special. That girl would squirm all over the place hotter than a stove. She'd do anything in the world just to get her own kicks. Later on in the day she'd just be a regular prostie again, no better than any of the others. But at ten in the morning she was really something."

"Was she pretty?"

"Not bad," Keith said. "Big in the breasts and broad in the beam. Her face wasn't the greatest thing in the world but it wasn't so bad that you couldn't stand to look at it."

"Is she still in business?"

Keith shook his head. "Dead," he said. "She was a junkie. Took an overdose of heroin and conked out. It was a shame."

"I thought heroin addicts didn't have sexual desires."

"They generally don't," Keith said. "This one was an exception. Jesus, what an exception! One time a friend and I both went to see her. You know, first thing in the morning. And, naturally, both of us wanted to be first because of the way she was. We were going to toss a coin, I guess, but she had a better idea. One we never would have thought of."

"What was that?"

"She wanted to take us both on at once."

"Really?"

"Honest to God. It was quite a deal, especially with her so excited. It's a shame she died. She was a good little whore. In the morning, anyhow."

They reached Saint Nicholas Avenue and crossed 125th Street, heading uptown. At once Dave saw the change in the area. Now, for two blocks, the streets were thick with girls. Here and there a white man could be noticed, usually with one of the girls on his arm. It didn't take a tremendous amount of perception to realize that the street was a cruising place for prostitutes.

Actually seeing the girls had a noticeable effect on Dave Forrester. Now, for some reason, he was unaccountably nervous. He wanted not the pleasure of making love to one of the girls but simply to get it over and done with as soon as possible. The memory of Sheila came up at him hard and he wondered if there was something wrong with him. Maybe it would happen again—maybe he would reach a quick and desperate climax before he had a chance to do anything. Or maybe he wouldn't be able to get excited at all.

Skillfully Keith piloted him to the corner of 126th Street. A girl approached them, very openly, and put her hand on Keith's arm. She smiled.

"You want some love, honey?"

Dave stared at the girl. Her skin was a dark brown, her hair long and black and glossy. Her face was pretty—a long and slender nose, white teeth, a pretty mouth.

Her body was even better.

The dress she wore, a sheath of flaming scarlet, was designed with two thoughts in mind. In the first place, it had to show her body as thoroughly as possible so that the customer would know what he was getting. In the second place, it had to be easy to get into and out of in a hurry.

The girl was not wearing anything under the dress. Dave could tell. Her breasts were huge and they did not need a bra. They jutted out against the sheer fabric of the dress and Dave could see the nipples very clearly. Her hips looked eminently functional. Already he could feel desire begin to course over him in a warm wave of passion.

"Well, baby?" The girl was talking to Keith. "I can be good to you, baby. Give you anything you want. I go any way in the world. I even go around the world, lover. You ready to play or am I wasting my time?"

Easily Keith dropped one hand on the girl's shoulder. His other hand roamed over her body, giving the firm breasts a squeeze, touching the hips, rubbing the stomach. The girl stood there patiently while he touched her.

"Baby," she said, "this ain't a free day. You know what I mean? And it's play for pay and pay for play, baby. Are you in or are you out?"

Keith smiled. "Well?" he said to Dave. "You interested?"

He nodded. "How much?"

"Hell," the girl said. "You pimping for him or something? Can't he bargain for himself?"

"How much?"

"Fifteen."

Dave would have paid the fifteen instantly. But Keith was evidently an old hand at the game.

"Five," he said.

"Five!"

"Ten then."

"Ten and he pays for the room."

The girl shifted her attentions to Dave. She rubbed her breasts against him, while with one hand she touched him.

"You don't mind," she told him. "Ten for me and two for the room. That ain't too much, is it?"

"Ten," Keith said positively. "And you pay for the room. Eight for you and two for the room."

"That ain't a hell of a lot."

"It's enough."

The girl shrugged. "Hell," she said. "Not much way I can get rich with guys like you around, is there?"

Keith smiled.

"C'mon," she said to Dave. "You want to go a round after him or what?"

"I'll find a girl on my own," Talbot said. "Dave, I'll meet you back on the corner when you're done. Good enough?"

Dave nodded. Then the girl took his hand and he followed her into the hotel.

•   •   •

The hotel was very obviously nothing but a cathouse for freelancers. A thin light-skinned Negro with a pencil-line mustache sat at a desk in the hallway with a register at his side. He looked up when Dave and the girl approached. His eyes smiled.

"Two dollars," he said pleasantly.

Dave paid him.

"Now sign the book."

The Negro passed the register open and handed Dave a ballpoint pen. Dave stood for a minute, not knowing what to write. He was momentarily lost.

Then, feeling very awkward, he scrawled *John Smith* in the space provided.

The Negro looked at the entry. "Better make that Mr. and Mrs.," he suggested.

Dave changed the entry.

"Thanks very much, Mr. Smith," the Negro said. "Bet we had some of your relatives staying with us tonight. You'd be amazed how many people we get named Smith. Getting to be a more popular name every day."

The girl laughed and Dave blushed.

"Take 1-D," the man said. He handed a key to the girl. "Have fun, people."

Then the girl was taking him by the hand and leading him down a corridor. He stood with his face hanging out while she opened the door with the key. Then they went inside and she closed the door and locked it.

Something, he felt, was very wrong about the whole thing.

It was so sterile, so businesslike, that something important was missing. It hadn't been like that with Sheila. That had been better, cleaner, fresher.

This was . . . commercial.

"What's your name?"

The girl stared at him. "What difference does it make, baby? A name is a handle is all. You got to know my name? Makes no sense."

"My name's Dave," he said awkwardly.

"Well, mine's Millie. Whatever difference it makes. You want to give me that money now?"

He took out his wallet, counted out eight dollars and handed the money to her. She counted them herself, folded them twice and tucked them into a pocket in her dress.

"Why don't you give me a little more?" she coaxed. "I'll be extra good to you."

He shifted nervously. Keith, he knew, would not give her an additional cent. But Keith had experience that he lacked. For some unaccountable reason he wanted the girl to like him, to be nice to him. It didn't make any sense. She was only a whore—in a day he would forget what she looked like. He was buying her—or, more accurately, renting her—and he sure as hell didn't have to look in her eyes for approval.

"Come *on*," she said. "Be good to me and I be good to you. That's fair, ain't it? Anything you want, little man. Anything in the world. And I won't make you hurry, either. You can take your time and we'll have a ball."

Ashamed of himself, he took out his wallet again. He handed her two more dollars and she put them away.

"Let's go," she said. "Get your clothes off."

He unbuttoned his shirt and pulled it out of his pants while she very speedily tugged her dress over her head and kicked off her shoes. She stood there, naked and evidently unaware of her nakedness, while he stared at her body.

She had the kind of body that ought to be naked all the time. Her breasts were long and shapely, twin turrets of warm brown flesh just a shade lighter than the rest of her. The nipples were very large.

Her stomach was flat and her hips were wide. He knew that he was staring but he couldn't help himself.

"You never see a girl nude before?"

He felt himself blushing.

"Come *on*," she said. "Get your clothes off, huh? Time is money, baby. You know?"

He started to turn away from her while he removed his clothes. Then he realized how ridiculous that was and stopped himself. He removed all his clothing and took a very hesitant step toward her. His hand reached out for her breast.

He didn't know where to begin. She was a whore, a woman bought and paid for, and it seemed ridiculous to stroke her, to kiss her, to make love to her. Besides, he had read somewhere that whores wouldn't let a customer kiss them. But what was he supposed to do? He wished he had stayed back at the dormitory.

There was a strange light in the girl's—Millie's—eyes.

"Baby," she said, "ain't you ever had a woman before?"

He blushed again.

"I don't believe you ever have," she said. "Baby, that ain't anything to be ashamed of. Hell, you're scared green, aren't you?

Don't you be scared of me. I'll be good to you, I swear it. No kidding, it's good luck to get a guy's first time. I'll make the first time so good you'll never forget it. Now you come here!"

Obediently he came close to her. She led him to the narrow, sagging bed and made him lie down on it. Then she stretched out next to him.

For the first time he noticed the odor of the room. It reeked with the extremely individual stench of stale bodies. The bed smelled, and he wondered how many men and women had used that bed for their lovemaking.

"Baby—"

He turned to Millie.

"You touch me," she said. "You play around with me, you hear?"

He touched her breasts. They were very firm, much harder than Sheila's had been. He squeezed gently, pinched the nipples, stroked the firm flesh.

But nothing was happening. Somehow, although he wanted to make love to Millie, nothing approaching desire came over him. The whole business was too much a business. His mind was tied up in knots and his body wasn't responding the way it was supposed to. Things were not going right.

He wanted to laugh. After he'd worked up a hell of a sweat, now when the chips were down, he was striking out. It was a hell of a note, all right. He wondered how he'd be able to face Keith afterwards. Keith would be able to tell, and he could never hold up his head again in front of the older boy.

"Baby, something the matter?"

"I . . . can't," he said.

"What do you mean?"

"I just can't *do* anything."

"You been drinking?"

"Just one glass of beer."

"That ain't it," Millie said. "Not just one glass. Must be that you're scared or something. No call to be scared of me, baby. All you got to do is relax."

It was easier said than done. Once more he tried to interest himself in her body, stroking her breasts and her flanks.

Again, nothing was happening. Nothing at all.

"You come here," she said positively. "Nothing wrong with you that I can't take care of. Told you it was going to be good for you and no fooling. You just lie down on your back, you understand? Just lie back and stretch out and close your eyes. I'll take care of you."

"Like this?"

"That's the ticket. That's the boy. Now you relax and enjoy it, you hear?"

He waited. Then he felt her hands on his chest, touching him deftly, moving over his body. Her hands worked their way down, touching very lightly.

"You relax," she cooed to him. "You relax, baby. Everything's roses."

Then she was kissing him, her warm mouth kissing the side of his neck, working her way down over his chest.

Meanwhile her hands were busy, touching him, caressing him, and his mind reeled with the impact of a dozen exhilarating sensations. He forgot himself, forgot his name, where he was, forgot everything but what the beautiful girl was doing so thoroughly to him.

"Nice little baby," she murmured. "Nice little baby. Millie's gonna take care of you, baby. Gonna turn you into a man. Gonna make you feel like a skinful of coke, little baby. Gonna make you see the top of the moon."

And then she was doing it.

Her lips—opening, moving forward, then closing over him and engulfing him.

More.

More . . .

He had never imagined anything could feet so good. But it did, it felt wonderful, and amazingly enough he began to respond to the sensations that her lips provided, the wonderful flow of passion transmitted from her to him.

Strength.

Manliness.

Power.

"There now," she was whispering. "See? I told you you could make it, baby. Now you come with me. You're ready now. Climb on and be good to me."

He moved instinctively, his eyes still closed, and he rolled on her perfect body, and they came together.

Her hips rolled with a movement as old as the hills, as old as the world, as old as Millie's profession. The bedsprings creaked in mechanical agony and the room rocked around them. He forgot that she was a whore and that he was a customer, forgot that he had been ashamed and embarrassed and afraid, forgot everything except that she was a woman and he was a man.

His mind reeled and the sweat poured out of their bodies. They were locked together, locked in a fast and furious combat that was bigger than the room, bigger than the hotel, bigger than the city, bigger than the world.

They were straining together, straining to reach the very heights of physical passion. Daggers of flame, hot from every corner of the room, swallowing them and engulfing them in white heat. The world swooped, veered to one side, disappeared.

He felt her go tense all at once. Then, simultaneously he stiffened to the ultimate point of tension. The wave soared to the crest.

And broke.

He rolled free of her, his arms heavy as lead. He felt drained, empty . . . and strangely filled with new life.

"Baby—"

He turned to look at her. He was sitting on the edge of the bed trying to get his underwear on. His hands each held five thumbs and he was having trouble.

"We can go again," she was saying. "For five more dollars we can have another trip to the moon and back again. What do you say, baby? We'll celebrate in style, you dig? To the moon and back again for a small five dollars."

He didn't say anything. He got dressed, got his shoes on and his shirt and pants on, got the pants buttoned and zipped and the shoes tied, and then he reached for his wallet. He took out a five dollar bill and handed it to her.

"Silly man," she said. "You had to put your clothes all on again and now you got to take 'em right back off. Or do you want me to take 'em off for you?"

He shook his head.

"Huh?"

"The five is ... for you," he said. "I don't want to do it any more now. Maybe some other time."

Her eyes narrowed. "You mean you're just giving me the five outright?"

He nodded.

"Hell," she said. "You come back and see me, you hear? You come back."

"I will," he said.

But he knew that he would never see her again.

Keith Talbot was waiting for him at the corner. Dave tried to look nonchalant and wondered if he was succeeding.

"Well?"

He shrugged.

"You were in there long enough," Keith said. "Was she any good?"

"Good enough."

"You have a good time with her?"

"I'm not complaining. How about you?"

Talbot shrugged. "I'm not complaining either," he said. "God, the one I got was homely as sin. Flat-chested, missing a few teeth, thin—"

"Then why did you pick her?"

Talbot smiled mysteriously.

"If she was that bad—"

"Looks aren't everything," Keith said. "Especially with the lights out. Then they all look the same anyhow. This one had special qualities that endeared her to me."

"Huh?"

"Let's just say that there are certain things she would do that not many girls will do."

"What?"

"Forget it," Talbot said. "The hell with it. We came to get laid and we got it. Let's go have a couple beers. I'll do the buying this time around."

Talbot took his arm and steered him across the street to a small dimly-lit bar. A neon sign announced the name of the bar in blinking green light. The bar was called the Green Door.

"Is this safe?"

"The beer's good."

"I mean . . . we won't get knifed or anything, will we?"

Talbot laughed. "Harlem's the same as any place else," he said. "There are places where you don't go, but the same goes for a white section. You can relax, Dave."

Heads turned when they walked into the Green Door; men and women stared at them. But when Keith led him to the bar and they took stools, oblivious to the people watching them, the heads turned away.

They ordered beers and drank them. Then Keith insisted upon buying another round, this time shots with beer chasers. Dave could feel the liquor going to his head. He had never been much of a drinker and he knew he couldn't hope to compete with the legendary Keith Talbot in that department.

Finally they left the Green Door and tumbled into a cab. Keith had an apartment off-campus so they dropped Dave off at his dorm first.

"Hang on," Talbot said. "You're a good man to go whoring with, Forrester. A damned good companion. You like the libertine life, don't you?"

Dave shrugged manfully.

"Nothing to be ashamed of," Keith insisted. "Drinking and loving never hurt a man. Good liquor and good women—you can't beat them. You know, you might be just the man I'm looking for. It's possible."

"What do you mean?"

Talbot sighed. "Look," he said, "suppose I told you there was a way for you to have all the sex you wanted without paying for it. Would you be interested?"

"Anybody would be interested. But come off it. You're not *that* drunk."

"I'm serious," Talbot said. "There's a . . . club, you might call it. Male and female members. Some of the membership might come as a surprise to you."

"A . . . *sex* . . . club?"

"Bad term," Talbot said. "Call it a society of libertines. A cult of mystics devoted to the pleasures of the flesh. Would you be interested?"

"I'd have to know more about it."

"Sensible answer," Talbot said. "Suppose we get together tomorrow night and talk it over. Good enough?"

He started to agree, then remembered Jan Chatterton. "Hell," he said, "I've got a date."

"Anybody I know?"

"A freshman girl. I don't think you'd know her."

Talbot chuckled. "A little libertine experiment of your own, eh? Good enough. The night after, then. At my place. Right?"

"Right."

"And Dave—"

He turned around.

"Forget everything I said to you," he said. "About the club. Until the night after tomorrow. Okay?"

Dave Forrester nodded and headed for his room.

CHAPTER 3

His dream that night was very long and very involved. He drifted off to sleep remembering how it had been with Millie, and the next thing he knew he was dreaming that he was running in a dark, moist cavern, running as fast as his legs could carry him. But he had no idea what he was running from. All he realized was that whatever it was behind him, it was absolutely imperative that he escape.

He ran on and on, and the cavern seemed to go on well nigh forever. It grew darker and darker until it was pitch black and he could see nothing in any direction. Still he ran on, periodically bumping into the walls of the cavern, then straightening himself out and racing forward once more.

Then he saw light at the end of the passageway. He hurried, driving himself faster and faster, and the cavern gave way to a patch of very green grass surrounding a deep and placid pool. He looked up and saw the sky. It was blue and cloudless, and when he looked down once more at the pool he saw that it was the same color blue. The waters of the limpid pool parted suddenly and a girl appeared. She swam around for a moment or two, then pulled herself up on the bank and stretched out on the green grass.

She smiled to him, and he saw that she was naked and very beautiful, her hair the color of autumn wheat, her body a collection of ripe curves. Her skin glistened with drops of water and her eyes glowed with mute passion.

She opened her arms to him, lay back waiting for him, and he went to her.

Then, all at once, the girl changed. Suddenly she was Millie, Millie the whore, and she was shouting to him.

"Money," she called. "Money, honey. Be a good baby and pay me. Money, honey."

And just as he reached for her, the nameless faceless horror burst forth from the mouth of the cavern and fell upon him. He tried to scream but he couldn't . . .

Bill Jergens, his roommate, had to shake him awake.

"Time to get up," Bill was saying. "You got to register for classes. Good God, I looked at your schedule. You didn't even make it out yet. What the hell were you doing last night?"

"Went out for a couple beers. Why?"

Bill shook his head. "Better move it, Dave. The registration line's going to be a lulu this year. I'm on my way there now. You better shake a leg."

He yawned, then lowered himself from the top bunk to the floor. "Hang on," he said. "I'll go down to breakfast with you."

"I already had breakfast."

"Christ! What time is it, anyway?"

"A few minutes after ten."

"Why didn't you wake me before?"

"I tried to. You were dead to the world. I had to check your pulse to make sure you were alive."

Dave shook his head. "Well," he said, "I guess that kills breakfast for the day. Wait up while I get some clothes on and we'll go to the registration line together."

"Can't."

"Why not?"

"I've got to rush, Dave. I'll see you."

Jergens left and Dave shrugged sadly. Well, that meant he had time to take a shower. He grabbed soap and a towel and hurried down the hall to the john. The shower spray was hot and it brought him back to life. He toweled off quickly, then got back to his room, dressed in khakis and a white shirt, filled out his proposed course schedule in less than five minutes, and left the dorm for the administration building.

Registration was always hard to take and became perceptibly worse on an empty stomach. He went from one endless line to the next, surprising himself by getting all of the courses he had wanted. Two of the courses were part of the required general education program which the college urged upon its students in an effort to develop well-rounded idiots; the other three were courses in his field, which meant that they just might be somewhat interesting.

With registration out of the way he finally had a chance to grab a bite to eat. It was after two by then, and the school cafeteria had been closed for over an hour, so he walked down Broadway to a luncheonette and ate there. The food could have been worse, perhaps, but outside of the school cafeteria he couldn't think of a place that made a habit of serving worse food. The hamburger was a greasy slab of cardboard served on a soggy bun. The French fried potatoes were greasier than the hamburger, and were quite raw in the middle. The coffee tasted like lukewarm battery acid mixed in equal parts with the same crankcase oil in which the potatoes and the hamburger had been cooked.

He had two bites of the hamburger, two of the potatoes, and three sips of the coffee. Then he paid the check and walked out without leaving a tip.

He only had around five dollars left in cash, but fortunately the school bookstore was willing to cash checks for college students. His book bill came to a staggering total of thirty-three dollars, making him wonder if perhaps majoring in biology wasn't a tactical error. The trouble with it was that science textbooks cost so goddamned much. If he'd had the good sense to room with another biology major they could have shared textbooks and halved the cost, but he hadn't been that clever. Jergens was a philosophy major, and all they shared was the room.

He lugged the books back to his room and was pleased to discover that Bill was nowhere to be found. He checked all of the books, writing his name and room number on the flyleaf of each, and then browsed through the textbooks and the course syllabi. The two required courses made up in simplicity what they lacked in interest, and he knew that at least they wouldn't monopolize much of his time. If he attended each of them once a week he could nail B's in both, possibly A's with a little solid studying. At any rate, they wouldn't waste his time too much.

The three field courses were a little different. Organic Chemistry for one, was going to be hell on wheels. Invertebrate Biology would be interesting and not overly difficult, and Ecology, a strange course bringing a sociological approach to biology, looked fascinating. He breezed through the syllabus, frankly interested, and decided that if the course lived up to the syllabus it would be more than worth whatever time he had to spend on it. The textbook was fairly impenetrable, loaded with terms that sailed handily over his head. But, with a good professor at the head of the class, he felt confident that he could handle the work.

Momentarily bored, he put the books on the shelf, found a record and got it going on Bill's hi-fi. The record was modern jazz, a very complex thing featuring Thelonious Monk, and he clambered up on his bed and stretched out on his back with his eyes closed, letting the music engulf him. He followed the strange chord patterns, paid close attention to the stabbing, strident piano that Monk played against the solos of the horn men. It was good music and he let it take control of him.

Suddenly he found himself thinking about Keith Talbot. He tried to decide just how he felt about Talbot, and had trouble making up his mind. He didn't dislike him now, and yet he wasn't able to say that he liked him. There was something vaguely sinister, almost evil about Talbot. He simply wasn't the sort of fellow one generally liked.

That, he told himself, firmly, was ridiculous. Talbot had been a damned fine friend the night before, giving him a hell of a fine helping hand. Maybe the reason he distrusted Talbot was that Talbot knew so much more than he did, had done so much more, had had so much more experience with women.

But now he himself wasn't a virgin any more—and the difference between himself and Talbot was a difference of degree rather than a structural distinction. Hell, wasn't a guy like Talbot a better friend than a square like Bill Jergens? He tried to imagine

Bill confronted with a hot naked squirming girl. The image was ludicrous and he felt like laughing out loud.

Bill wouldn't know what to do. He'd probably quote some passage out of John Locke and then turn tail and run like a rabbit.

Not Dave—not any more.

And certainly not Keith Talbot.

Then he remembered what Talbot had said in parting. A strange conversation, to say the very least. How had it gone?

Suppose I told you there was a way for you to have all the sex you wanted without paying for it. Would you be interested?

Would he? God, of course he would. Anybody who wouldn't must have something radically wrong with him. But what else had Keith said about it?

Call it a society of libertines. A cult of mystics devoted to the pleasures of the flesh. Male and female members.

Keith Talbot, he decided, was putting him on. No club like that could exist. Why, if the college found out about an organization like that, it would be all over for the members.

But suppose the college *didn't* find out?

Suppose the club just went on, without anyone but the members ever discovering a single fact pertaining to its existence? Suppose there really was a club, and, it really did work?

It was fantastic.

And it was just barely possible.

He tried to imagine what it would be like. A group of guys and gals, meeting together and having sex. He wondered where they would meet. Talbot's apartment? He'd never been there, but he was willing to bet it wasn't big enough for meetings of that nature. Well, maybe they had something like a fraternity house, a place where they held their meetings.

Fantastic.

But, again, possible.

And he had a chance to join!

Well, if Talbot hadn't been talking through the top of his head, and if the club really existed, and if he really had a chance to join, he knew damned well what his answer was going to be. He remembered how it had been with Sheila, up to the incredible disappointment. Then he remembered how it had been with Millie.

Then he combined the two and the combination was out of this world. A girl like Sheila Reeves, warm and crawling the walls for him.

And performance like Millie. Except for free, because the girl wanted it too.

He took a deep breath and let it out slowly. For a moment he tried to imagine his parents' reaction to something like this. They would be horrified, he knew, and he supposed it was fitting and proper for them to be horrified. In a sense, a club where sex was on the menu was quite horrifying.

But in another sense, he decided that it was only fitting and proper for him to join the club—if it existed. His parents had sent him to college to get an education, and a club like that would give him an education in the fullest sense of the word. An education in his major field of interest, too. All the lectures in the world couldn't give him the basic biological experience afforded by such a club.

And, after all, he *was* a biology major.

The record ended and he climbed down from the bed and took it from the hi-fi, returning it to its jacket and slipping it into place in his record rack. He looked at his watch and discovered that it was almost time for dinner. Then, suddenly, he remembered his date with Jan. What was her last name? Not Chatterbox, but something like that.

Jan Chatterton.

He felt like seeing her. And he didn't feel like eating alone in the cafeteria. Not now, not after missing breakfast and eating three bites of lunch in that greasy spoon. He felt like a good meal at a decent restaurant, and he needed company.

That would cost money, so first he found a guy in the hall who would lend him ten bucks. Then he found a phone and put through a call to Kallett Hall. He asked the girl on the switchboard for Jan Chatterton.

A moment later the girl answered.

"This is Dave Forrester," he said. That was the last thing he had a chance to say for a moment, because the girl seemed determined to live up to her nickname.

"But it's not eight o'clock yet," she said. "And I suppose that means you're calling to break the date, and I think that's perfectly horrible of you. Especially since I've been running around like a chicken with its head cut off all day long, and I've been looking forward to seeing you, and even if I did practically force you to ask me out it still seems as though you ought to be enough of a gentleman to keep the date once you made it. Of course it's probably something important that came up and I understand, really I do, even if I am disappointed. So if you want to make it for another night, well, that's fine with me, and anyway I can always spend tonight studying or something, although there's nothing much to study because my classes don't start till tomorrow, and—"

"Hey!"

She paused for a moment and he seized the opportunity.

"I'm not breaking the date," he said. "I called to ask you if we could make it for dinner and then take in a show or something. That's all."

"Dinner?"

"Dinner."

"Like at the caf?"

"Like in a restaurant."

"Where?"

"There's a great Chinese restaurant a few blocks from here. I thought we could go there."

"Like chow mein and chop suey?"

"Definitely not," he said. "North China food. Like pressed duck with chopped almonds and things like that. It's pretty great stuff. Sound okay?"

"Sounds wonderful."

"When can I pick you up?"

"Well," she said, "it'll take me a few minutes to get dressed and everything, so don't come right away. And I'm sorry I blew up at you like that, because I know I was awfully nasty but I thought you called to break the date and I really wanted to see you so I assumed . . . but you know what I mean and anyway I have to go now and get dressed so I'll look pretty for you and be ready when you get here and—"

"I'll see you," he said. And hung up.

While it didn't seem entirely proper to hang up on a girl, he didn't see any other way to get off the phone. He walked back to his room whistling happily, stripped down and got dressed in a paisley shirt and a pair of light-weight gray flannel stacks. He hesitated, then decided he might as well do it up brown and added a thin black tie and grey tweed sport jacket that matched the slacks nicely. Then, still whistling, he left the dormitory and headed slowly across the campus for Kallett Hall.

She was waiting for him, which was something. And she was wearing a dress, and this was also something. When he had met her the night before she had looked like a kid—a hell of a fine-looking, well-developed kid, but a kid nevertheless. Now, in a dress and high heels, she looked like a woman.

A hell of a woman.

She talked a blue streak on the way to the restaurant. She told him what courses she was taking, and what her roommate was like, and what town she was from, and what her father did for a living, and how many brothers and sisters she had, and a good many other things that she managed to think of, most of them uninteresting. But, while her conversation was not too exciting, the girl herself was fairly fascinating. There was a natural warmth to her personality that was delightful, and when the personality was added to her face and figure, the girl resulting from the mixture was a rare and wonderful girl indeed.

He decided that he liked her.

The meal at the Shanghai Pagoda lived up to the sales talk he had given it. First they had the inevitable bowl apiece of wonton soup. Then, however, the restaurant revealed that it was not the usual chop suey joint. The waiter came, beaming, and spread a bed of rice on each of their plates. Then he placed casseroles before them and lifted the lids triumphantly. Inside large chunks of pressed browned duck topped with ground almonds nestled on a heavy layer of pungent lettuce. They spooned the duck onto the rice, saturated the result with sweet jelly, and began to eat.

And for once Jan Chatterton was appropriately silent.

"Delicious," she said, after the last bite of almond cookie had been washed down with the last cup of tea. "Simply delicious. I'm at a loss for words."

"I guess that doesn't happen very often."

"Hardly ever. You're nice, Dave Forrester. Where do we go from here?"

"That depends," he said. "Do you like foreign movies?"

"Sometimes. What's playing?"

"There's a good Swedish film at the Little Art Theatre," he told her. "*A Sound of Distant Drums*. It's directed by Ingemar Schwerner."

"I've heard of him," she said. "I saw one of his pictures once. It was a little tough to understand but I liked it."

"Should we go, then?"

"Let's," she said.

They went.

A Sound of Distant Drums was not an easy picture to understand. It was, as a matter of fact, an almost impossible picture to understand. The photography was excellent, the acting amazingly good, and he enjoyed it very much—but he was damned if he was sure what the whole thing was about. The title was seemingly irrelevant, but he had to admit that it was a nice title. Had a good ring to it. Sounded fine.

They held hands during the movie. It was corny, maybe, but it was nice. There was something so very fresh and sweet and honest about her that it touched him. At one point he had an insane desire to tickle the palm of her hand, just to see what would happen, but he restrained himself.

Later they had coffee together at a lunch counter. "That was fun," she said. "I don't think I understood the symbolism, but I enjoyed it."

"So did I."

Silence.

"Say," he said after a few minutes had passed. "What's the matter with you? Are you sick or something?"

"No," she said. "Why?"

"You haven't been talking a mile a minute lately. I thought something was wrong. As far as I can tell, you never keep your mouth shut for more than a minute at a time."

"I don't always talk that much."

"No?"

She shook her head. "Only when I'm nervous," she said, "or scared or something."

"And you were scared with me?"

"I am with almost everybody."

"And you're not nervous any more?"

"No," she said. "Not any more."

They walked back to her dorm in silence, holding hands, walking very slowly. He was glad to be with her, glad to walk her home, and at the same time he began to have sexual thoughts about her. He looked at the front of her dress and wondered what it would be like to wrap his hands around those big boobs of hers.

He didn't want to think things like that—she was a nice girl and he liked her, and sex could wait.

But he couldn't help thinking about it.

She was a virgin—he was sure of it. And she was a virgin who would be anxious to hang onto her virginity. Not until marriage, not necessarily, but until she was in love with somebody and certain that he was in love with her. She wasn't a girl to seduce.

But he wanted to seduce her.

The best thing, he decided, was to go on dating her but not to push things too hard. He'd kiss her for awhile, and in time, if one thing led to another, he'd settle himself in the saddle and have the ride of his life.

In the meantime, he could wait and play things cool. If Talbot's sex club really existed, he'd have plenty of outlets for his newly-developed manhood. Jan Chatterton would be taken care of, but there was plenty of time before he had to worry about deflowering her. Plenty of time.

He walked her to her door.

"Well," she said, "I had an awfully nice time."

"We'll have to do this again soon," he said.

"I'd like that."

He smiled. "This is going to be a busy week for both of us. How's Saturday night?"

"Sounds fine."

"I'll call you," he said. "We'll find something to do. Okay?"

"Okay."

She looked at him, and he knew that she wanted him to kiss her. Well, he decided, the coolest move would be to play a waiting game. But at the same time he didn't want her to think he wasn't physically attracted to her.

So he took her face between his hands, brought her close to him, and kissed her lightly on the forehead.

Then, before she had time to know what to think, he had turned and left.

Classes started the next day, and they were a pain in the neck. His field courses, the interesting ones, were scheduled for Monday, Wednesday, and Friday. The required bit, garbage of the worst order, was set for Tuesday, Thursday, and Saturday. Since the first day of classes was a Thursday, he had to suffer through an hour of Fundamental Concepts of Mathematics and Basic Principles of Economics.

The math course, appropriately dubbed Moron Math by the student body, was an ill-conceived cross between logic and ad-ministrative accounting, sort of a philosophical approach to basic arithmetic. The economics course, similarly known to the cogno-scenti as Ec For The Idiot, was simply a simplification of a sim-plification of a simplification, and consequently a monumental drag.

The day passed slowly.

The night was a definite improvement.

After dinner—a hasty meal of mangled veal and vague-ly-boiled potatoes dished out in the cafeteria—he looked up Keith Talbot's address in the student directory. Talbot lived at 711 West 113th Street, and Dave went there at once, wondering what sort of a place a person like Talbot would live in.

It was an impressive building. Located on the corner of 113th and West End Avenue, the building was red brick and seven stories tall. A uniformed doorman stood in the entrance-way, but he seemed to be decorative rather than functional. Dave walked right past him, looked up Talbot's apartment on the building's directory, and took the elevator to the fifth floor.

He rang Talbot's bell.

He waited for a moment or two, shifting his feet and thinking that it might have been a good idea to call Talbot before coming over. For all he knew, Talbot had completely forgotten the invitation. He might have a girl in there, for all Dave knew, and if he did he certainly wouldn't appreciate Dave's coming over and leaning on the bell.

But Talbot didn't have a girl in there. He opened the door, looking rather royal in a purple smoking jacket and brown suede slippers, and beckoned Dave inside.

"Glad you could make it," Keith said. "I wasn't sure whether you were coming over or not. I was just about to give you a ring, as a matter of fact."

"Well, here I am."

"So you are. Come on in—have a seat. It's not much, but it's home."

The apartment was small—a room, a kitchen, a bath—but it made up in luxury what it lacked in size. A thick carpet covered the entire floor of the living room. An expensive-looking couch unfolded to become a bed for sleeping, and for other indoor sports as well. An elaborate hi-fi system occupied one corner of the room and a bar took up another corner.

"Can I get you a drink?"

"If you've got a beer."

Talbot nodded, walked to the kitchen, then reappeared with a cold can of ale. "No beer," he said. "But this should do just as well."

He sipped the ale while Keith poured bourbon over ice for himself. Then Talbot came over and sat next to him on the studio couch.

"I suppose you're wondering just what this is all about," he said. "I was mysterious the other night, and you probably don't know what to make of the whole thing. For all you know, I was exaggerating something or making up a complete batch of lies. Right?"

"Well—"

"Naturally," Keith said. "You'd be a damned fool if you didn't have your doubts. Now, before I explain, tell me what I told you the other night."

"Don't you remember?"

"Not entirely. I'm not sure how much I said."

"You said there was sort of a libertine society with male and female members and that a member got as much sex as he wanted free of charge."

"That's quite correct."

"Well—"

Keith took a drink. "Let me start at the beginning, okay? The club is known as the Libertines. Just that, no phony symbols, no Phi Upsilon Kappa, none of that. Just the Libertines. It was founded in 1924—"

"What!"

"In 1924," Keith repeated. "Surprised? Well, it's a fact. The club's been rolling along for quite awhile now. We have twelve members, no more, no less. Four each from the sophomore, junior and senior classes. Two men and two women. Each year four members graduate and four new sophomores are invited into the society. You, of course, will be one of the four. *If* you're interested in joining."

"It sounds pretty fantastic," Dave admitted.

"Hell, it *is* pretty fantastic. Here's the set-up: We meet once a week, every Friday night, at a building on Spring Street. That's a few blocks south of Greenwich Village. The building is officially vacant. The club owns it. Four-story building in a nonresidential neighborhood. Completely private."

"Go on."

Keith shrugged expressively. "What more is there to say? We meet, watch an occasional movie, pair off and follow our inclinations. The club house is well-equipped with a film library, an unusual record collection, and some rather bizarre albums of photographs as well as a stock of erotic reading material. There are beds in all the rooms. You go there, amuse yourself, find a girl, and amuse yourself some more. How does it sound?"

"Incredible."

"What part is hard to believe?"

"The house, for one thing. How does the club happen to *own* a house?"

"We've owned it for years," Keith said. "You've got to remember this is an on-going institution. Dues are fifty dollars a year, which is quite low. If a member has more money, he pays more. And then there are donations from past members who have a warm spot in their hearts for the society. One charter member sends us a thousand dollars a year. He runs a small manufacturing firm in New England and he has more money than he knows what to do with."

"Okay," Dave said slowly. "I'll buy that. But . . . who's in the society, for God's sake? It sounds so weird."

Keith shrugged again. "I could name names," he said, "but what good would that do? The girls are all beautiful, if that's what you want to know. And they're all available to any member, and not just on the nights when meetings are held. Any time you want to crawl into bed with one of the members, all you have to do is pick up a telephone and give her a ring. All of the members in the junior and senior class have apartments off-campus, naturally, to make things easier. You'll have one next year. You call your girl of the moment, tell her to come over or go over to her place, and you do whatever you feel like doing."

"That's not hard to take."

"You said it. You don't have to limit yourself to one girl, either. Every once in a while last year I would call up two girls for the same night. Then I'd crawl in the sack with both of them. Ever do that?"

Dave shook his head.

"It's a ball. I had one blonde and one brunette, both perfectly lovely. I'd fool around with one and then the other, going back and forth. Then I had them both, one after the other, and then I slept between them."

"God!"

"And you know what happened?"

"What?"

"I woke up and saw them having a go at it. The two of them.

Like lesbians, you know. They weren't lesbians, of course—just interested in experimenting a little. So I got up and showed them what a man could do, and then the three of us went right back to bed again."

Dave didn't know what to say. The conversation was getting to him, exciting him, and he knew that he had to join the club or go crazy thinking of what he was missing.

"Ever watch two girls go at it?"

Dave shook his head.

"Well, you know what they do, don't you? Lesbians, I mean. When they're in bed together."

"I've got an idea."

Keith chuckled. "Believe me," he said, "it's really something to watch them. Not just to watch them, but then to have them, one after the other. Makes you feel like a man through and through. It's quite a kick."

"I can believe it."

Keith finished his drink. "You in?"

"If you'll tell me why you picked me. I mean, I'm not a campus big shot or anything. I'm just an ordinary guy. How did you happen to hit on me?"

"Because you're a libertine."

"I am?"

"Of course you are. I could tell last night. You've got that hunger in you and it shows through. Oh, not everybody could see it. But I could. You're the type of person always looking for a new kick, a more exciting experience. That's the type of people we are, and that's why I invited you."

"I see."

"So you'll join?"

Something nagged at him. "I . . . believe you," he said. "But . . . well, it's so fantastic—"

"That you want proof."

"Well—"

Keith grinned. "In that case," he said, "I'll show you proof. You know Betty Stacey, don't you?"

"I don't exactly *know* her."

"But you know who she is?"

"God," Dave said, "everybody knows who she is. Senior girl, queen of the campus, prettiest girl in the school . . . you don't mean to say *she's* in the club, do you?"

Keith's grin widened. He held out an envelope, a brown manila one with a clasp.

"Open this."

Dave opened the envelope.

"Now look at the pictures."

He looked at the pictures. There were four of them, glossy nine by twelves, and the girl in each was unmistakably Betty Stacey. The pictures left no detail to the imagination. And Betty was not alone in the pictures. In each one she was with a boy, and in each she was engaging in a different variety of sexual embrace.

Dave stared.

"Like them? Quite a girl, that Betty. You can't tell from the picture, but the guy with her is me. We had a lot of fun making these shots."

"God!"

"Like her? Join up and you can have her any time you want. She's a lot of woman, Dave."

He stared at the pictures, then looked up at Keith. This was more than proof—it was an incredible incentive to join the Libertines, an incentive he couldn't pass up.

"I'm in," he said.

"You're sure?"

"Positive."

Keith Talbot beamed at him. "I figured you would," he said. "You better get home now, Dave. Get some sleep. The first meeting is tomorrow night and the initiation is pretty stiff. You want to be in shape for it."

"Initiation?"

"Sure."

"What's the initiation?"

Talbot took a deep breath. "I'm not supposed to tell you too much about it," he said.

"But—"

"I'll give you a clue. You'll be called upon to make love to three girls in three different manners."

"Three?"

Keith nodded. "That's why you have to be in shape for it. See? You shouldn't have much trouble. It's not as though you have to take on the entire Woman's Army Corps. Hell, it's just three girls—and you'll enjoy it. I'll guarantee it."

Dave nodded slowly. He had only made love to one woman in his entire life—Millie. And he had had enough trouble acquitting himself properly in that instance. How in the world was he going to manage three of them?

"Worried?"

"I suppose so. A little. You mentioned getting into shape. How do I do that?"

"Lots of sleep," Keith said. "Get right home, take a hot bath and hit the sack. Get all the sleep you can. A nap tomorrow afternoon wouldn't hurt. Got that?"

Dave nodded.

"Stay away from alcohol," Keith went on. "Worst thing you can have before something like this. Good to get a girl loose and easy, but no good for a guy. Knocks him on his ear. You know what the Bard said about it: *Lechery it doth both provoke and doth unprovoke. It provoketh the desire but taketh away the performance.* Shakespeare sure as hell knew what he was talking about. No liquor, no wine and no beer until the initiation is over and done with. Then you can drink all you want, but lay off the sauce until then."

"That won't be any problem."

Keith grinned. "It would be for me. Now there are certain foods you ought to eat—conditioning foods is what I call them. Lots of milk, first of all. And a thick blood-rare steak for dinner. And one thing more, if you've got the stomach for them. Half a dozen eggs an hour or two before the meeting."

"Six eggs?"

"Right."

"I hate eggs."

"Ever try 'em raw?"

Dave shook his bead.

"That's how you ought to eat them. Just crack them into a glass one at a time and pour them down your throat. It sounds pretty terrible but they aren't bad. And they'll get you through the initiation with flying colors."

"Well, I guess it's worth it."

"It is," Keith said.

"Raw?"

"Raw."

"Well, I guess I can manage it."

"Good man," Keith said. "Now, the meeting is at nine o'clock. The address is 190 Spring Street. You ring the bell three times short, then wait a beat, then three long. Got it?"

"Three short, wait, three long. 190 Spring Street."

"You got it."

"Why don't I go down with you?"

Keith Talbot shook his head. "The rest of us will be there early," he said, "setting things up for you and the other new members. You come down by yourself. And don't be late or we'll start without you."

"What should I wear?"

"It doesn't make a hell of a lot of difference. Whatever it is, you won't be wearing it very long. What you've got on now is fine. Now get the hell out of here, okay? You need your sleep and I've got something of my own to take care of."

He nodded and stood up. Keith showed him to the door and he rode down five flights in the elevator. His mind was buzzing with all the things that Keith had told him. He was planning and dreaming, thinking of the women he would have, the thrills and pleasures and forbidden joys he would taste.

His heart beat faster.

He was so preoccupied with his own thoughts that he barely

noticed the girl walk into the building as he left it. But he did notice her at last, because she was not the type of girl you failed to notice. Her flaming red hair fell far past her shoulders. Her eyes were a deep green. And her body was superb—long and slender, with magnificent eye-catching breasts.

He recognized her at once. And, although he would have recognized her regardless, he knew her instantly now.

He had seen her picture not long ago.

She was Betty Stacey, and she was on her way to Keith Talbot's apartment.

CHAPTER 4

Dave Forrester went to bed the minute he got back to his dormitory. First, of course, he followed Keith's instructions and took a hot shower. The shower made him sleepy, and although he thought he would be too excited to drop off to sleep, he was unconscious seconds after his head hit the pillow.

He awoke the instant the alarm clock went off, showered, dressed, and headed for breakfast. He had a large glass of orange juice, three scrambled eggs, and two big glasses of milk. He passed up both the usual cup of coffee and the cigarette that always went with it and headed off to his first class.

The classes held a certain amount of promise, especially the ecology course. But he couldn't pay too much attention to what the professors were saying. He was too busy thinking about the night ahead.

He ate lunch, a meal he had previously forgotten for the greater part of his life as a college student. Again he had two large glasses of milk, a fruit salad, and a dish of cottage cheese. There was something slightly hysterical about his diet, and as a biology major he could appreciate it. He was eating what an animal breeder would call *conditioning foods*—foods designed to put an animal in the proper shape for breeding.

He remembered when, years ago, he had had an aquarium

of tropical fish. His object all sublime for several years had been to coax a pair of dwarf gouramis into breeding. The gouramis, which usually got along quite handsomely on a diet of powdered fish food, required more elaborate preparation if they were going to honor his aquarium with their spawn.

So he had gone all out to supply them with the live food that would get them into shape. He had dug earthworms and chopped them up fine. He had tossed nets into foul-smelling marshes to gather live daphnia for them. He had even bred guppies and fed the baby fish to the gouramis.

And, finally, success had crowned his efforts. The male dwarf gourami had made a little nest of bubbles in one corner of the tank, and the female had coyly joined him. Little eggs were released by the female fish, and the male gathered them in his mouth, put them in the bubble nest, and fertilized them. In a few days half the batch hatched, and Dave was the proud father of half a hundred baby dwarf gouramis. Conditioning, he was convinced, had been the answer.

And conditioning was going to be the answer for him. He would be in flawless breeding condition, and when he was called upon to perform with the three girls, he would give a commendable performance. Then he would be a full-fledged member of the Libertines, with all the rights and privileges of a member.

Privileges like Betty Stacey.

He spent the afternoon lying in his bunk with jazz records on the hi-fi and a book in his hand. The book was the ecology text, but he wasn't paying too much attention to it. He didn't want to tire his mind. He merely thumbed through the textbook, reading a page here and a line there, and resting up, saving his strength for the ordeal ahead.

He had dinner in a Broadway steakhouse—a thick sirloin so rare it was barely warm, a baked potato dripping in melted butter, a portion of spinach. He wondered if the Popeye legends were true. Probably not, he decided. According to what he'd read spinach was mostly water with a little sand added. But it couldn't hurt him. He passed up dessert, skipped coffee, and refused to permit himself even the luxury of an after-dinner brandy. Then, at a quarter to eight, he went to a food shop around the corner and bought a dozen eggs.

He took the eggs back to his room, cracked them one at a time into his water glass, and poured them straight down his throat. The first raw egg took a certain amount of nerve, but after that the going became considerably easier. He managed to finish seven of them before he got the definite feeling that one more would cause him to heave up all of them, and the steak and baked potato as well. He tossed the rest of the eggs into the wastebasket and left the dormitory room.

At 8:30 he decided that it was time to head downtown to the meeting place. He got on the West Side IRT train at 116th Street, rode it to 59th Street, and changed to the double-A IND which he rode to the Spring Street stop. Then he got out of the train station, lit a cigarette to quiet his nerves, and began to look for number 190 Spring Street.

He found it quickly enough less than a block from the subway station. It was an ancient red-brick building four stories tall and it looked vacant, or at least harmless. There was nothing visible from the outside to indicate that the building was used for anything as exotic as meetings of the Libertines. On the left was a machine shop, an iron gate stretched across its entrance. On the right were the twin quarters of a shoe repair shop and a Chinese laundry. And in the middle was Libertine headquarters.

For an insane moment he wondered whether Keith Talbot had sent him on a wild goose chase. But that was impossible. The pictures of Betty Stacey, the presence of Betty at Keith's apartment after he himself had left it—these factors indicated beyond any shadow of a doubt that Keith was telling the truth.

He stepped up to the door of 190 Spring Street. His finger found the bell, hesitated.

Then he rang three short rings, paused for a moment, and rang three long.

It was Keith Talbot who answered the door, Keith Talbot with a smile on his face and a glass of amber liquid in his hand. He extended the other hand to Dave.

"Come on in," he said. "You're right on time. I'll introduce you to the other members."

He followed Keith up a flight of stairs to the main room, which seemed to be on the second floor. On the way Dave studied the building itself. The inside was far different from the outside, lavishly furnished in Edwardian decor, with heavy furniture, wood paneling, wine-colored draperies and built-in bookshelves. The place looked like nothing so much as an old English club, where the members drank lukewarm scotch and soda and read their copies of the London *Times*.

Then they were standing in front of a heavy oak door. Keith opened it and motioned Dave inside.

There were seven people in the room. With Keith, they made up the full membership of the Libertines. Dave stared blindly around the room, astounded by the membership.

Avery King, editor of the *Record*, the campus newspaper, was present. His thick eyebrows were raised and a slight smile graced his thin lips. He was supposed to be the most brilliant student in the college, as well as the most singularly venomous. His editorials were thinly-veiled darts that stabbed in all directions. Dave had never thought of the thin, nervous editor as a Libertine. Now, seeing him there with his arm around Mary Stackpole, he seemed to fit in perfectly.

Mary Stackpole was stacked, if not Polish. She was a very tall, willowy girl, and her huge breasts seemed out of place with her long and leggy body. But nobody had ever complained about them. Now King was squeezing her breasts, and Mary seemed to be enjoying the act immeasurably.

Betty Stacey was there, of course. She was sitting in a corner with Jeff Cruikshank, a tackle on the football team. Jeff had his hand up her skirt, and they both were evidently quite preoccupied with what they were doing. Dave wondered idly how Cruikshank was able to play top-notch football while breaking training in such a magnificent manner. The stocky tackle was evidently one hell of a man all across the board.

"Jeff and Betty you know," Keith said. "And Avery and Mary. The blonde over there is Leila Morse, and the guy with his hand inside her sweater is Marty Pekorsky."

Leila was a platinum blonde, and Dave was willing to bet that her hair had come out of a bottle. He wasn't complaining, how-ever, because the effect was excellent whether her hair was nat-ural in color or not. Why Marty Pekorsky bothered to put his hand inside her sweater was another question entirely. Leila was a damned fine-looking girl, but her chest was indistinguishable from that of a boy.

"And this gal here," Keith said, pointing to a short brunette with lots of eye makeup, "has been waiting for me. Her name is Sandy Wilkins and she's a doll."

She was.

"How about the other new members?" Dave wanted to know. "Aren't they here?"

"They're all here," Keith said. "Each of them is in a separate room waiting for the initiation to start."

"What kind of initiation do the girls have?"

Keith laughed. "Harder than yours and easier than yours all at once," he said. "They have to take care of all four male members. But that's easier, in a way, than it is for a man to make love to three girls. A woman can just go through the motions without being particularly excited, whereas a man has to be physically interested in what's going on. Hell, I don't have to explain it to you. You're a biology major. I don't have to draw pictures for you."

Dave laughed.

"Okay," Keith said, "you've met the members. Now come with me. I'm your sponsor, so I have to get you ready for the initiation. Right this way."

They climbed another flight of stairs, and Keith led him down a dimly-lit hallway to a room. He opened the door with a heavy brass key and led Dave inside.

The room had a rug on the floor and a large double bed right in the middle of the room. There was no other furniture.

"Here's the field of valor," Keith said. "You stay right in here. When you're ready for the first girl, press a bell. She'll come in and tell you exactly what you have to do to her. When she's finished, rest until you're ready for the next one, then press the bell again. Same with the third."

"How long can I rest?"

"Up to you," Keith said. "But if more than two hours elapse from the time the first gal walks in until you're finished with the last one, then you don't qualify."

"Two hours!"

"That's right. It's not as hard as it sounds, believe me. The main thing is to use your head. Don't take too much time with any of the girls. You don't have to prove to them what a hot lover you are. Just get it over and done with so you conserve your energy as well as you can."

"I see."

"Remember, don't try to be a hero. This is a pretty tough initiation, although I don't doubt that you can handle it. You'll have these girls as often as you want once you pass your initiation. Just concentrate on taking care of all three of them."

Dave nodded. By now he was impatient to get started. He wondered which girls he would get. There were only four, and he would have three of them. Let's see—there was Betty Stacey, Mary Stackpole, Leila Morse and Sandy Wilkins. Which ones would he have?

"I'm going now," Keith Talbot said. "Sit for a minute or two, let yourself relax, get undressed, then ring the bell. And good luck, Dave."

"Thanks."

Keith opened the door, walked outside, and closed it behind him. Now Dave was left alone. He took out a cigarette, tapped it twice on the back of his hand, then changed his mind and returned it to his pack. Somewhere he had heard or read that tobacco could interfere with sexual potency, and he didn't want to take any chances. Three women in two hours! It seemed impossible. But he had to get started, had to do as well as he could.

He got undressed, piling his clothing in a corner. Then, at precisely fifteen minutes after nine, he rang the bell. He would have until 11:15 to fulfill the requirements.

The door opened and Mary Stackpole walked into the room. She was wearing a jet black cocktail dress that dipped almost to her navel. Her bra, which was plainly visible, was a wisp of black lace with red fringe. She was wearing plain black shoes with very high French heels.

He stared at her.

"Hello," she said. "I'm going to be the first with you. I'm glad of it, you know. I like to be first. And I think it ought to be good with you. You've an excellent body, you know. You're quite well equipped."

He felt like blushing.

"What . . . are we supposed to do?"

She had a slight English accent which he was quite sure was an affectation. But he didn't mind it. He liked her.

"We are supposed to make love," she said.

"How?"

"In the usual manner. Don't worry—you'll be getting a sufficient amount of variety with the others. You won't *mind* making love to me, will you?"

"Hell, no!"

"Then come on. You might begin by undressing me, if it's all right with you."

She turned her back to him and he walked to her, his finger trembling. He felt ridiculous in his nakedness, but when his hands worked the zipper on her dress he felt a good deal better. He ran his hands down her bare back. She was taller than he was, and her skin was smoother than satin.

"The bra, please."

He removed the bra as well. The dress fell to the floor and she stepped out of it. She shrugged her shoulder and the bra fell off. Then his arms went around her slender body and his hands cupped her huge breasts. Her breasts were not merely large: they were actually oversized. He had never so much as seen a girl built like her. He cupped her breasts and fondled them and wished he had larger hands.

"That's nice," she said. "That's very nice."

Gingerly she disengaged his hands and turned around to face him. She wore only her panties and her high-heeled shoes. The panties matched the bra—wispy black lace, and scarlet fringe that swayed when she moved.

He could see right through them.

"Kiss my breasts," she said.

He lowered his head to each breast in turn, kissing her red

nipples. It was obvious that she enjoyed what he was doing, but her passion was entirely different from that of any other woman he had ever met. It was an extremely contained sort of passion. She didn't writhe, didn't squirm, didn't moan. And yet she was very definitely excited, and also very exciting.

"Take off my panties."

She stood as still as a statue while he pulled lacy fringe-covered panties over her hips and down her perfect legs to the floor. Then she stepped out of them rather daintily, stark naked except for the jet black high-heeled shoes. He had never seen heels so high before.

"Touch me."

He wanted to make love to her slowly, so slowly that he could penetrate that icy British reserve of hers and make her cry out at the top of her lungs in sheer desperation. But there simply wasn't time. Time was precious: he had only two hours to make love to her and to two other girls as well, so he could not afford to do what he wanted to do to her.

She was extremely acquiescent. She stretched out on the bed, lying on her back, and he was astonished to discover that even in such a position her breasts lost none of their firmness. They stood up straight and solid, and his hands held them and squeezed them with passionate fury.

It was a strange sort of lovemaking. In a sense, it was like making love to a corpse. She did not move to meet his passion with passion of her own, did not strain for her own culmination, did not thrust with her hips or grind her every essence into his.

But, in another sense, she was an extremely passionate girl.

He sensed that every movement he made drove her to greater heights, just as it filled him with thrills and heat, white heat that burned through his young body with an ice-blue flame. He could feel the excitement mounting within her, could feel her reaching and moving closer to the peak.

Some day, he knew, he would make her cry out in agony. He would tease her again and again, raising her toward nirvana and stopping inches short of the goal, until she squirmed like a snake and begged him.

But there was no time now.

So he sweated and strained, surging toward the climax. His body went tense as a bowstring and the world began to race past him at top speed.

The sky grew dark and clouds covered it. Slowly, then faster, the clouds turned to blackness and the sun was blotted out entirely. The clouds moved in the churning motion of a tornado, spinning like a dervish.

Blacker and blacker grew the clouds, as his blood surged through his body and his heart pounded against his ribs. He could not see and he could not hear. He could not touch and he could not smell and he could not taste.

The world raced by. The clouds were blacker than night, and he felt her breasts beneath him, supporting him, and her legs cushioning him. His body rose and fell, and he knew that it was going to happen, that it was as inevitable as death and taxes, that no force on earth or in heaven could possibly hold back what had to come.

The clouds opened up.

The rains came.

And he fell forward upon her perfect body, spent and exhausted and empty.

He was still on the bed, still gasping for breath, when she got up without a word and began to dress herself. He was exhausted, unable to move, and he knew that he had made a mistake, that he had put entirely too much of himself into their lovemaking. He wondered if he would have sufficient strength to handle two other girls, and he didn't see how he could do it.

"That was good," she said to him, as if she was teacher and he was a pupil, anxious to please. "That was very good," she said. "We'll have to do it again some time when we don't have to hurry so much."

Then she was gone.

He looked at his watch. It was almost a quarter to ten.

He rang the bell again at five minutes to ten. When Mary Stackpole had left, pushing her huge breasts in front of her like antennae, he had not thought he would feel like making love to another woman for at least several hours and more probably for several days. But he failed to take into consideration the preparation he had undergone for his ordeal. The raw eggs, the milk, the steak—all had done something to him that had made one hell of a man out of him.

And, when he rang the bell that second time, he was ready for anything. He hoped, of course, that the woman who came to him would be Betty Stacey. As far as he was concerned, she was easily the most desirable woman in the world. Everything about her murmured of sex, and to look at her was to want her desperately.

But the girl who came to him was not Betty Stacey.

The girl was Leila Morse, with the platinum blonde hair.

She was happy.

"Hi," she said. "You're Dave—right?"

"Right," he said, grinning.

"I'm Leila," she said. "And I'm terrific."

"I'll bet you are."

She was wearing a sweater, a black cashmere one that hugged her boyish chest. Her slacks were also black and very tight, and she was barefoot. She pirouetted neatly on one foot, and he saw that whatever curves her chest lacked were more than compensated for by her behind. She had a magnificent rear end and he wanted to pinch it.

"No time to waste," she chirped. "You've got one more girl after me, and I know what a headache this initiation business can be."

"Well, I wouldn't exactly call it a headache."

"All right," she said giggling. "So it's another part of your anatomy that aches. Believe me, I know what these initiations are like. I went through one just a year ago. Four boys, and each more determined than the last. They have a contest when they initiate the girls, you see. They see which one can make it last the longest. You may not believe this, but when I was initiated one of the boys did it for over an hour. I thought it was going to last forever. God!"

He could imagine.

"So let's get this over as quickly as we can," she said. And she suited her words to her actions, stripping her sweater over her head and peeling off her black slacks. She did have breasts after all, he discovered. They were tiny, but they were there.

And her hips and behind were lovely.

He was sitting on the edge of the bed and she threw herself into his lap, wrapping her arms around his neck.

"You like me?"

"Uh-huh."

"Then play with me. Look at me and touch me and feel me a little."

"Sounds like fun."

"*Is* fun. Look, I bet you think I don't have natural platinum hair. Right?"

He blushed.

"If you check," she said, "you'll find out that I don't dye my hair."

He checked and she was right.

"Touch me," she said. "Fool around with me. I love it."

He was in a hurry.

"I've got something better to touch with than my fingers," he said. "Why don't we do the job properly?"

"Can't."

"Why not?"

"The initiation."

"Huh?"

"You did it that way with Mary," Leila said. "You have to do it a different way with me."

"How?"

"You have to use a different place."

"Where?"

She showed him.

"There?"

She nodded. "It's lots of fun."

"I never did it."

"You'll like it," she said. "It's called Greek style. You know the joke, don't you?"

"Which joke?"

"You know," she said, squirming around in his lap. "The nightclub comic comes on and says how he had a lot of trouble on his wedding night. Then he says *My wife was a Greek girl and she didn't know which way to turn.*"

"Oh," he said.

"But we better hurry," she said. "There's not much time left. Let's get on with it."

He was a little dubious about it, but he held her close and kissed her. Then she turned away from him and crouched on the bed.

"Touch me," she said. "Warm me up."

He stroked her smooth flesh, marveling at her perfection. She had the most lovely rear end he had ever seen.

"Kiss me," she said.

"Like this?"

"Oh, that's right. Oh, that feels good. Now do it. Come on, Dave. Do it hard and fast."

It began, and he was surprised to discover how enjoyable that variation could be. Her whole body flexed and swerved with him, tripling his passion, making everything that much better for him.

And throughout it all she knelt before him and kept up a steady barrage of words, never stopping, never ceasing.

"Oh," she moaned. "Oh, Dave—it's so good but it hurts so much. It hurts, it hurts, God how it hurts. Dave you're hurting me, you're killing me, it's like a flaming sword and it's killing me."

He wanted to stop, to release her from her agony, but he couldn't. He was too excited himself now, too excited to stop for a minute, for a fraction of a second.

The passion was out of control now. He moved with her, and the world spun, and it was happening.

And he fell away from her, out of breath and totally, thoroughly exhausted.

"I'm sorry," he said at last.

"Sorry?" She looked at him, her eyes mirroring her amazement. "What do you mean, you're sorry? What in the name of the lord are you sorry about?"

"I'm sorry I hurt you."

She stared at him.

He remembered what she had said, the hurt sounds she had made. He remembered the scream of pure pain that had burst forth from her lips at the moment of truth when the sheer evidence of his potency had surged forth.

"It hurt you," he insisted. "You were moaning. And what you said—I *know* it hurt you."

She didn't say anything.

"And that's why I'm sorry," he said lamely.

"Dave," she said.

"What?"

"Don't be sorry."

"Why not?"

"Because I loved it."

"But . . . it hurt you, didn't it?"

She nodded.

"Then—"

"Dave, I *wanted* you to hurt me."

"But—"

She sighed. "You don't understand," she said. "I have what they call masochistic tendencies, I guess. I don't know why, but I do. And I like to be hurt. When you were . . . doing what you did to me, I thought I was going to die from the pain. It was horrible. I was in agony."

He didn't say anything. He simply did not know what he was supposed to say.

"And I loved it," she went on. "I always love it when it hurts. It's much better for me then. The more painful it is, the more it hurts me, the more I like it."

He had read about girls like Leila. He had heard of men and women who liked to be beaten, whipped, hurt. But he had never imagined that a girl like Leila had tastes like that. For a moment he was sickened.

Then he realized that he was being a prude. The Libertines were supposed to be people with an interest in the exotic, the bizarre, the unusual. His own role was one of which society would disapprove, and it was certainly not his place to cast aspersions on the desires of another member. To each his own. *De gustibus non disputandum esi.*

"You're surprised?"

"A little," he admitted.

"It just happens to be my particular kick," she told him. "Everybody has his own kick. This is mine."

He nodded.

"I'm going to get dressed now and get the hell out of here," she said. "You don't have too much time and there's one more girl to go yet. Just lie there and relax, Dave. Save your strength."

He watched her dress and leave. He looked at his watch.

It was a quarter to eleven.

He had only thirty minutes to go and he was too tired to move. His hands shook. He couldn't fail now, couldn't miss out at this stage of the game.

But what could he do?

Well, he had to try, had to make an effort. It was better to die trying than to simply lie there and fail.

His head was reeling and his palms were moist with his own perspiration. He took a deep breath, tried to stand up, and almost pitched forward onto his face. Grimly he steadied himself and reached for the bell. He rang it, hoping at least that the last girl would be Betty Stacey. If the lovely redhead came to him, then maybe he would have a slim chance. Not much of a chance, but a slight and slender one.

The door opened.

And Sandy Wilkins entered the room.

She was stark naked.

•　　　•　　　•

"I wanted to save time," she explained. "You don't have much time left. I didn't want to waste any of it taking off my clothes. I hope you don't mind."

He most definitely did not mind. The girl was very lovely— short but shapely. The eye makeup made her dark eyes look even larger than they were. Her hair was very long, and she had it arranged so that it fell over her wide breasts. Pert pink nipples peeped through between the strands of black hair.

"Let's get to work," she said. "Let's finish up your initiation. There's not much time."

"I . . . don't think I can do it."

She laughed. "That's what you think," she said. "I'm something of an expert, I'll have you know. I can excite any man in the world, and you're no exception."

"Maybe," he said, "but—"

"No buts."

"I just don't think I can do it."

She came over and sat down next to him. "You just don't understand," she said. "You've never done it with me before. You don't know what I'm like."

Her hands ran over his body and she went on talking. "I'm going to do something to you that nobody ever did before. I'm going to do something you never even heard of or read about or dreamed of. It's going to be the most exciting thing you've ever experienced, and you're going to get excited. Believe me, this never fails. It's like magic. It's the most wonderful thing that can possibly happen to a man."

He wondered what she might be talking about. Maybe she

meant what Millie the whore had done to him several nights ago. But he was sure that wouldn't work now, not the way he felt.

"You don't believe me," she said, "but you'll see. You'll see what it's like."

He shrugged.

"Now relax," she told him. "We only have a little time left. You just relax and I'll do all the work."

Then she began to do it to him.

And she was right—it was something he had never done, had never dreamed of, had never heard of or read of. It was incredible, impossible to believe, impossible to describe. It was the most unimaginably exciting thing in the world.

Sensations flooded over him. His exhilaration knew no bounds, and colors swam in his head, thoughts burned through his fatigued brain.

It was amazing.

"See?" she demanded. "Isn't it great?"

It was.

"Isn't it the most wonderful thing you've ever felt in your whole life?"

It was.

And it went on and on and on and on, lifting him to heights he had never before reached, never before dreamed of. And it seemed to be working.

"It's working," she was saying to him now. "It's working and it's getting there and I told you you didn't have a thing in the world to worry about. There, now. There, see? See what happened to you!"

"But will it last?"

He was worried.

"Of course it will," she said. "Now see what we're going to do. See? Isn't this divine?"

And it was, because they were making love in an incredible, unbelievable way, a way that sent his pulse racing a mile a minute. He knew now that everything was indeed going to be all right, that he was going to pass his initiation with no difficulty now, that he would be a Libertine and that he had nothing at all to worry about from here on in.

It got better.

And better.

And better . . .

And the world raced by a third time, and the world fell apart at the seams a third time, and he knew that it was happening, happening, happening . . .

And that was all he knew. The world went black and he slipped into unconsciousness, fell headlong on the bed. His eyes closed and he blacked out.

And slept.

He awoke just a few moments later. Marty Pekorsky was shaking him by the shoulder in an attempt to wake him and Keith Talbot was grinning and slapping him on the back.

"You did it, Dave! You made it!"

He smiled.

"Now you're a Libertine," Keith was saying. "A member in good standing with all the rights and privileges of membership. You'll have to cough up fifty skins eventually, but don't worry about that for the time being. The important thing is that you made it. You're in like Flynn."

Dave shook his head groggily. Pekorsky handed him a small glass of brandy which he downed at once. It helped. Then he lit a cigarette, drew smoke deep into his lungs, and felt a good deal better.

"How about the others?"

"The other guy finished already and went home. The girls are still busy."

"Who was the guy?"

"Clark Reynolds. You know him?"

Dave nodded, surprised that Clark was in the Libertines. He knew Clark fairly well, had been in his Freshman English class. Clark was quiet, soft-spoken, the type of person who disappeared in a three-person crowd.

"How about the girls?"

"You probably know them as well," Keith said. "Elaine Rice and Sally Chen."

"Sally Chen!"

Keith grinned wickedly. "That's right," he said. "And take it from me, brother, it's true what they say about Chinese women. Whatever they say, it's true."

Dave shook his head in amazement. Sally Chen had also been in one or two of his classes. She was a lovely Chinese girl, with exquisite features, small bones, and lovely eyes. He tried to imagine what it would be like to go to bed with her. Well, he would find out. He would find out everything.

And Elaine Rice was certainly no let-down herself. Her family owned land in Virginia, lots of it, and qualified as one of the grand old families of the Confederacy. But if Elaine was an example, the virtue of Southern womanhood was vastly overrated. Elaine was one of the three girls Dave had dated during his freshman year. He had been only a lowly frosh at the time, so a goodnight kiss was all he had managed to get. But it was no secret that half the student body had been getting into Elaine Rice.

Now it would be his turn.

"You probably want to get home and sack out," Keith suggested. "The first meeting of the year is never a regular meeting, anyhow. We have the initiation and then we break up. A week from tonight we'll have a full-fledged meeting—movies, maybe even a demonstration or two."

"Demonstration?"

Keith winked. "You'll see," he said mysteriously. "Anyhow, we'll meet at 8:30, same place. You can come by yourself or bring one of the member girls down with you. That's strictly up to you. The main thing, of course, is to disclose the existence of the society to no one. Don't even drop hints about it. And it goes without saying that you can never bring a non-member to a meeting of the society."

Dave nodded.

"I guess that's it," Talbot said. "You're welcome to stick around as long as you want tonight, but I have the feeling that you're a little bit tired."

"That's an understatement."

"That's what I figured. You should look at yourself in the mirror, my boy. Bags under your eyes and hanging half way to your navel. You're a mess."

"I put in a hard day's work."

Keith threw back his head and laughed. "All work should be like that. Let's see—you had Mary and Leila and Sandy, in that order. Right?"

"Right."

"Aren't they great? That Sandy knows some pretty amazing tricks. Take my advice and spend a whole night with her sometime. She can keep a man awake every minute of the time. You don't get a chance to shut your eyes for a second when that little piece is in bed with you."

Dave could believe it.

"I think I'll go now," he said finally. "I am pretty tired, and there's nothing I feel like doing. Sexually speaking, that is. So I'll fall in a cab and go home."

Keith walked him to the door.

"Don't forget," he said, "you're a member now. You can call any member girl anytime you want and have her do whatever you want her to do. Of course, the obligation works both ways. Any of the girls can call you and have you come over."

Dave sighed heavily. "I hope they don't call for awhile," he said. "It may be a few days before I'm the least bit interested again."

He walked away with Keith Talbot's laughter ringing in his ears.

CHAPTER 5

To say that he had no trouble getting to sleep that night would be the understatement of the century. He rode home in the cab with his eyes closed, then paid off the cab driver and staggered up to his room. He tore off his clothes, threw them in the general direction of the closet, climbed into his bunk and slept the sleep of the dead for twelve magnificent hours. He woke up the next afternoon at 1:30, having slept through the two required classes, and he felt wonderful.

He wrapped himself up in a towel, picked up a bar of soap and headed down the hall to the shower. His skin still smelled of sex, and he washed himself thoroughly, rubbing the bar of soap all over his body and letting the lashing spray of boiling hot water bake the taste of dissipation from his flesh. He soaped again, then rinsed again, then turned off the hot water entirely and permitted an icy jet of cold water to bring him back to life again. Then he left the shower, toweled himself dry, and made his way back to his room.

He dressed in a hurry, took a good breakfast of waffles and bacon in one of the better Broadway luncheonettes, and followed the breakfast with three cups of good black coffee. The coffee got his brain turning over once again, and he headed back to his dormitory room to put in a heavy session at his books.

For the first time in a long time he was able to apply himself fully to his academic work, concentrating more thoroughly than he had ever been able to concentrate in the past. He pored over the Moron Math textbook, raced through sample problems, until after an hour and a half of concentrated studying he was in a position to cut the class for the next several weeks. The next hour and a half he devoted to economics, with similar results. The material that he studied was material that he learned quickly and permanently. He had no difficulty in digesting it and he felt secure in his belief that it would remain with him permanently. The three hours he put in that afternoon were the most productive hours of study he had ever experienced.

It wasn't hard to see what was responsible for his increased efficiency. He realized at once that because he was sexually satisfied he was able to free his mind completely for academic work. For a short time he had worried that joining the Libertines would entail a sacrifice scholastically, but now he was discovering that quite the reverse was true. His membership in the Libertines would be an actual boon to his scholarship.

At five o'clock he closed the economics textbook and sat back yawning. He had a date that night, a date with Jan Chatterton, and he had to call her to tell her when he would pick her up. He decided not to make it a dinner date. For one thing, he was going through money much too quickly. For another, he wanted to play things very cool with the girl. He thoroughly intended to seduce her, but he was in no great hurry. The girls in the Libertines would supply him with sufficient sexual outlets. Jan Chatterton could wait her turn.

Well, where could he take her, then? Not another movie—there had to be something better to do than that. Maybe Greenwich Village, he decided. She was from out of town, a freshman, and the Village would probably impress the hell out of her. Besides, it wouldn't cost a hell of a lot. Fifteen cents apiece each way on the subway, unless he decided to splurge on a cab coming home. A quarter apiece for a cruddy cup of coffee in a cruddy coffee house. And not a hell of a lot else.

He left his room and headed for the phone in the hall when he bumped into a hall-mate.

"Phone," the hall-mate said. "For you."

He decided it must be Jan, wondering what had happened to him. So he walked to the phone and said hello to it.

"David?"

It didn't sound like Jan Chatterton.

"David, this is Betty Stacey. I met you last night, but unfortunately we didn't have the chance to spend any time together. I was very sorry about that."

He couldn't talk. He could barely breathe. Betty Stacey was actually calling him, asking him to come to her. It was hard to believe.

"You seemed very nice," she went on. "On the strength of that one meeting, that is. And several of the girls had very nice things to say about you. I'm looking forward to getting together with you, David. I was wondering if you could come over tonight."

He started to say yes. Then, hysterically, he remembered the date with Jan Chatterton.

"I'd love to, Betty," he began. "But . . . well, I have another date for tonight."

"I see."

She sounded disappointed.

"It's with a freshman girl," he continued. "I made it quite awhile ago and I don't see how I could break it."

"With a freshman girl?"

"That's right."

"Just a . . . casual date?"

He knew what she meant. "That's right," he said. "Just a casual date."

"The girl will have a curfew," Betty said. "You'll have to bring her home early."

"I guess so."

"Would you like to come over afterwards?"

His heart jumped. "I'd love to."

"Fine," she said. "Do you know where I live?"

"No."

She gave him an address in the West 80s and he committed it to memory. "Don't be late," she said. "That is, don't be any later than you absolutely have to. I'll be waiting for you."

The phone clicked in his ear.

He stood there, numb, imagining what it was going to be like with Betty Stacey. As far as he was concerned, she was easily the most beautiful girl in the world. Her skin was white and satiny, her hair long and red, her body rich and luscious. He thought that in a very short time he would be learning the secrets of that body, rejoicing in the pleasures of her succulent flesh.

When he had returned from the initiation he had thought that it would be a long time before he wanted another woman.

He had been wrong.

Already he wanted Betty Stacey, wanted her with a passion

that frightened him. His palms itched, craving to hold her big breasts. His mouth was suddenly dry.

He wanted her.

Ached for her.

Yearned for her.

Keith was right, he decided. He was a libertine at heart, a libertine from his toes to his ears. He was one of those people who simply couldn't get enough, and he definitely belonged in the society. Without it he would be lost. With it, with women like Betty Stacey at his disposal night and day, he was quite literally sitting on top of the world.

He remembered the pictures Keith had shown him of Betty Stacey. She evidently liked variety in her lovemaking. And he would give her whatever she wanted. He would keep her busy all night long, quenching whatever strange thirsts her body held, satisfying her entirely.

And then, with the image of Betty Stacey's naked body still etching itself firmly into his feverish brain, he lifted the receiver to his ear, hesitated for a moment, and put through a call to Jan Chatterton.

A hall-mate of hers answered the phone, a girl with a particularly harsh voice. The harsh voice told him to for God's sake hang on a minute, which he for God's sake did. He waited, and then Jan's voice came over the phone to him.

"This is Dave," he told her. "How's everything?"

"Okay," she said. "What's new with you?"

"Nothing much," he lied. "Say, we've got a date going for tonight, haven't we?"

"Uh-huh."

"Let's see," he said, trying to give the impression that he was deciding where to go on the spur of moment. "Have you ever been to Greenwich Village?"

"Never."

"Like to go?"

"I'd love to. I've heard a lot about it. It isn't dangerous or anything, is it?"

He laughed. "Hardly," he said. "A little bit of a clipjoint, maybe. But as safe as your own campus. However safe that may or may not be."

"Then let's go," she said. "I was sort of hoping you'd say it was dangerous, so that I could be a little bit scared, wouldn't you say? But I'd love to go. What time will you pick me up? And what should I wear, and everything."

"You must be nervous."

"Me? What makes you say that?"

"Your conversation. You're clipping along at about a mile a minute. You told me you only do that when you're nervous."

"Oh," she said. "I'm sorry."

"Don't be sorry. Suppose I pick you up about eight, maybe a few minutes earlier. Good enough?"

She said that would be fine, and he was glad. The earlier he picked her up the earlier he could bring her home. And the earlier he brought her home, the sooner he could get over to Betty Stacey's apartment.

"Don't dress fancy," he said. We don't want to look like tourists if we can help it. Wear a pair of slacks and a sweater. No heels on the shoes."

"Okay," she said. "I'll see you around eight. It sounds like fun."

•   •   •

It *was* fun.

He picked her up at her dorm and discovered that she was just as much of a knockout in slacks and a sweater as she was in a dress and high heels. They rode downtown to Sheridan Square on the IRT, then wandered east to Washington Square where they listened to an Italian play a mandolin and sing sad songs. Old men played chess on stone tables and wild-eyed youths beat the bejesus out of bongo drums in the circle at the foot of Fifth Avenue. Dave and Jan ate Good Humors and sat on a park bench and talked.

Then he took her on a Cook's Tour of the Village, wandering through narrow twisting streets. He pointed out jewelry shops and leather shops and coffeehouses and bars and restaurants. They stopped for a drink at a bar where a piano player belted out blues chords. They watched sidewalk artists sketch pictures at a dollar a throw.

And they had fun.

They wound up at a small and secluded coffeehouse deep in the west Village, a dark corner of the world known as Ariadne's Web. There they sipped demitasse cups of bitter black espresso coffee and talked in whispers.

She had to be back at her dormitory by one o'clock, and he made sure they got her home in plenty of time. They took a cab back, and she sat close to him all the way. When they crossed 42nd Street he put his arm around her and drew her still closer. She lifted up her face to be kissed and his mouth found hers. He was amazed at the softness of her lips. She kissed like a little girl, her lips close together, her eyes closed.

He kissed her several times. Then, suddenly, they were at 116th Street and he was paying off the cabdriver and walking her back to her dorm.

"I had a wonderful time," she said.

"So did I."

"We're a few minutes early, Dave. We could sit on a bench for awhile. Unless you're in a hurry."

He *was* in a hurry, but he didn't want to say so. He led her to a bench in the middle of the campus and he sat down beside her. This time she came to him with a little whimper, her mouth ready to be kissed. His arms wrapped around her and he held her very close, his lips gentle with her. When the kiss ended she snuggled her face against his chest and did not say a word.

They sat that way for a moment. Then he brought her face up to his and kissed her. This time his tongue forced its way between her lips and he French-kissed her. It was not hard to see that she had never been kissed that way before. It took her a few minutes of experimentation before she was able to get the hang of the whole thing. He wondered what corner of the universe she came from. A girl as good looking as Jan Chatterton didn't get through high school without getting kissed properly.

"I . . . never kissed like that before."

He wanted to tell her not to go into raptures over it. Instead he kissed her again, and this time she was decidedly better at it. Her mouth opened to admit his probing tongue. She licked his tongue with her own, holding him tight, and he could feel her breasts stabbing him through his shirt and her sweater.

Passion began to build within him. He wanted her now, wanted to rip off her slacks and sweater and take complete possession of her right there in the middle of the campus. He had to struggle to control himself. He told himself again that he had to be cool with her, that he couldn't rush things. Besides, he had Betty Stacey to look forward to. She would be a more adequate release for the excitement that Jan was generating.

"Dave, I never kissed a boy like this before. But no boy ever made me feel the way you do. I like you very much, Dave. Maybe too much."

"I . . . uh . . . like you, Jan. Very much."

He kissed her again. Then he dropped his hand to her breast and touched her. Almost instantly she pushed his hand away.

God, he thought, she was the most virginal thing in the world! He tried to imagine her at a meeting of the Libertines and he felt like laughing out loud. But at the same time there was a quality of sweetness about Jan that he couldn't help finding appealing.

"Don't touch me like that, Dave."

"I won't hurt you."

"It's just that nobody ever did and I'm scared."

"Relax," he told her. "Just relax. I promise I won't hurt you."

Then he began to touch her breast again, very gently. He didn't want to be obvious about what he was doing. He acted as though stroking her breasts was simply a friendly caress, but his fingers worked to arouse her.

And did a good job of it.

She began breathing heavily, and he could feel the heat mounting within her. She was sweet and virginal, all right, but he knew that she would be a tigress when he got her properly aroused.

But tonight was not the time.

Just as she began to grow excited he took his hand from her breast, kissed her quickly and stood up. "It's getting late," he said. "We don't want to get too involved."

He led her to her door.

Then he kissed her once more and made a date with her for Wednesday night. She was very happy, and he figured he could afford to give her two nights a week. After all, why not? He had five other nights of the week for sex. It wouldn't hurt to give Jan the other two.

Then she went inside and he raced across campus and caught a cab to Betty Stacey's apartment.

Betty Stacey lived on the second floor of an old brownstone on 84th Street between Columbus Avenue and Central Park West. He hurried up the stairs, his heart pounding, then waited outside her door for a moment or two to compose himself. He lit a cigarette, blew out the match, drew a cloud of smoke into his lungs, blew it out in a long thin column, and knocked briskly upon her door.

She opened it.

He had met her before, and he had seen pictures of her before, but the sight of her was still enough to take his heart and place it squarely in his mouth. Even if she had not been beautiful, the combination of her red hair and her very pale skin would have been striking enough. But she *was* beautiful, with perfect features and a perfect body.

"I'm glad you could come, Dave. Come on in. Can I get you a drink?"

He sat down on the couch in her living room while she mixed dry martinis for both of them. She handed him a glass, clinked hers to his, and they drank.

Her dress was green. It matched her eyes and contrasted vividly with her hair and her skin.

He could see that she was wearing nothing under it.

Nothing at all.

Nothing but her lovely body.

"I'm so glad you could come, David," she was saying. "I was very sorry I didn't have a chance to . . . get together with you last night. I would have enjoyed being with you for your initiation. It would have been nice."

"I'd have liked that."

"But," she said, "in a way I think this is better. Initiations are so hurried, so fast, so hectic. They're exciting enough in their own particular way, but a man and a woman can have a much deeper experience than an initiation can afford them. Don't you agree?"

"Sure," he said. "It was all rushed and everything."

"That's just it. Tonight we don't have to rush anything, David. Would you rather I call you Dave or David? I like the whole name better myself, but it's up to you."

"David's fine," he said. "When you say it."

"You're sweet, David. But as I was saying, tonight we have all the time in the world. We have no reason to hurry. We can go very slow and take our time and make it last forever. Then we can sleep in each other's arms. That will be nice, don't you think? I'd like to sleep with you."

He didn't know what to say.

So he kissed her.

He was unprepared for the violence of her embrace. The minute his lips touched hers, her tongue shot into his mouth and her arms wound tight around him. The kiss was enough to make him tremble with desire instantly.

"Let's go slow," she said. "There's so much time. I'll put a record on, David. We can dance. Would you like to dance with me? I think it would be nice."

They finished their drinks. Then, while he sat on the couch, Betty walked to the record player and threw a switch. Soft and vaguely hypnotic music suffused the room, wrapping them up in waves of sensual sound. There were speakers in every corner of the room, and the result was a bath of sound, a deluge of soft music that engulfed them.

She turned toward him, then kicked off her shoes and stood barefoot, waiting for him. He took off his shoes and socks and went to her, folding her in his arms.

He felt her body taut and warm and demanding against his. He stroked the back of her neck with one hand while he pressed her buttocks with the other, drawing her close to him. They danced so close they seemed like one person.

The dance ceased to be a dance. It was vertical lovemaking, with all of the subtleties of sexual combat. He closed his eyes and his head swam with excitement.

He kissed her lips, her eyes, her nose. He kissed her ears and she seemed to tingle with joy.

He bent over and kissed her throat, her shoulder.

They danced without moving their feet. Their bodies moved

while they stood still, and he plunged his tongue deep into her mouth and drank the very sweetness of her.

By the time the record ended he felt as though he was walking high in the middle of the air.

Then there was no music, and she was standing close to him, looking up at him. "The way you hold me," she said. "The way you look at me and talk to me. How do you think of me?"

"You're a queen." The words sprang from his lips.

"A queen?"

He nodded.

"That's very interesting," she said. "If you take a man and a woman and put them together, they play their parts. It all depends upon how they relate to one another. Sometimes the man will think of the woman as a tramp. Their lovemaking reflects this. Or they will be equals, and again their lovemaking is a reflection of this attitude. But you say you think of me as a queen. Why do you see me that way?"

He groped for words. "You're regal," he said. "You're like a . . . higher being. You're brilliant and beautiful and . . . I've just never met anybody like you. That's all."

"And would you like to treat me like a queen?"

"Yes."

She smiled softly. "I think I would like that," she said. "I think I know what I would like you to do to me."

"Anything."

"Wait here," she told him. He stood in his tracks while she disappeared into another room. Then she returned with a picture.

"Look at this," she said.

He looked. It was a picture of a man and a woman. The man

was doing to the woman just what Millie had done to him. It was something he had hardly ever thought of doing to a woman. He had considered it disgusting. But he realized now that this was the proper way to make love to a creature like Betty Stacey. She was a queen. She deserved the treatment accorded to royalty. She had to be treated like a queen.

"Would you like to do this to me?"

"Yes."

"Are you sure?"

"Yes."

"Because a lot of men don't like to."

"I want to."

"Have you done it to girls before?"

He shook his head.

"Then—"

"I've never met a woman like you before, either. That makes a difference."

She smiled contentedly. He stared at her and thought about what he was going to do. It would be good, very good, and then they would go to her bed and roll in one another's arms all night long. It would be heaven.

"Undress me," she said.

She stood absolutely still in the center of the room while he walked behind her and unzipped her dress. The zipper ran almost to the floor. He unzipped it and discovered that he had been right. The dress was all she had worn.

She stepped out of the dress. He picked up the green cloth and carried it to the couch where he put it down. Then he walked to her.

She had not moved.

He stood in front of her, staring at her. She was a symphony of colors—the flaming red hair on her head, the deep green of her eyes, the creamy whiteness of her soft skin.

"Now, David."

Quickly he took off his own clothing. She was the queen and he was her servant; although he had carried her dress and placed it carefully upon the couch, he was not careful with his own clothes. He let them stay where they fell.

Then he dropped to his knees.

"Start with my feet, David."

She stood motionless, regal, while he kissed her feet. He groveled before her, his lips touching each small well-formed toe in turn.

Then he kissed her ankles.

Then her calves.

Slowly his lips worked their way upward along the path to heaven. Her legs were as smooth as silk and he was amazed to discover how stimulating it was to kiss them. By the time he reached her lovely knees he was shaking like a leaf.

He kept going.

She did not move a muscle.

Higher.

Higher.

Higher.

And his lips were more insistent, and he came closer and closer to the part of her that demanded his attentions, his reverence, his obedience. He could feel the way she was responding to his fervent kisses, and yet her majestic body moved not at all. She was immutable, a statue of a goddess, whiter and purer than marble, softer and sweeter than cotton candy.

Closer.

Closer.

Her passion was evident and he could feel the thrills going through her, could sense her own excitement. He, too, was excited, almost unable to bear the joy inherent in what he was about to do. He held himself back as long as he dared.

Then he began.

The world raced by and she began to tremble like a leaf in the breeze, her whole body unable to remain steady.

It went on and on and on, and he felt the way her blood was racing at a breath destroying speed, and he kissed her and he felt it beginning for her. The full force washed over her, and he pressed to her and trembled with the joy he was bringing to his queen.

Then he stood up like a man in a dream, and her face was flushed. He looked at her and he wanted her so much that it hurt.

"David," she breathed. "David—"

He took her arm and she led him to the bedroom. The bed was large and had satin sheets. She lay down on the bed and held out her arms for him.

He went to her.

It was heaven, pure and simple. It was the existence and the essence, the beginning and the end, the world and the wild and the wasted. It was the naked and the dead, the cry and the covenant, the young and the wicked. It was pride and prejudice, sense and sensibility, heaven and hell.

It was Abbott and Costello, Gallagher and Sheean, Lord and Marshall. It was Tippecanoe and Tyler as well.

It was great.

They made love for hours, over and over, their urgent bodies coming together with the velocity of thunderclaps. Then they slept, and when they woke up the next morning they came together once more, half-drugged with sleep and half-blind with desire, taking new pleasure from each other, making the world soar with the intensity of their lovemaking.

That afternoon his roommate asked him where he had spent the night. He invented an aunt and uncle of his who lived in New York and said that he had spent the night there. The explanation seemed to satisfy Bill Jergens, but Dave realized that he was going to have problems on his hands if he didn't get out of the dormitory and into an apartment of his own in short order.

For one thing, there were only six girls in the club, and if he didn't have an apartment he'd be eliminating two of the six from his plans. Since both Elaine Rice and Sally Chen were sophomores and lived in dormitories, he couldn't expect to spend a night with them unless he had a place off-campus. And he fully intended to get them in the hay before too long.

It seemed pretty logical to him to get together with Clark Reynolds, the other sophomore member of the club. He looked up Clark in the student directory, saw that he lived in the same dorm two floors down, and dropped in to see him.

Clark had similar ideas himself, as it developed. They pored over the Real Estate section of the Sunday *Times*, looking for an inexpensive apartment in the area, and Monday morning they went out hunting.

Monday afternoon they got lucky. They found a two-room apartment on 11th Street near Amsterdam. The place was a mess, but they decided that it hardly mattered. The important thing was the cost. Since the apartment only ran fifty dollars a month, they realized that they could rent the place while living in the dorms. That would eliminate suspicion while giving them a place to bring their girls for the evening.

"You got anything lined up for tonight?" Clark asked.

"Not a thing. Why?"

Clark shrugged. "I figured we ought to baptize the place properly," he said. "Call up a pair of girls, have them over, knock off a bottle of wine or something and take the girls to bed. We could switch off, sort of. Each take care of our girls and then trade off. How does that sound to you?"

It sounded fine to Dave.

"I want that Leila girl," Clark said. "That platinum blonde. I didn't get a crack at her initiation night and I've been aching for her ever since. I hear she's a real blonde."

"She is."

"She's fine with me, then. She good?"

"Great."

"Fine," Clark said. "I'll call her, then, and tell her to buzz over about 8:30. How about you?"

"I think I'll try Elaine."

He called Elaine Rice, who was enthusiastic about the whole notion. They met, the four of them, and they drank chianti until it was coming out of their ears.

Then Clark went to bed with Leila. And Dave went to bed with Elaine.

He and Elaine made fast and furious love, after which the wine and the lovemaking acted as soporifics and knocked him on his ear. He dropped off to sleep, and when he awoke the girl next to him was Leila.

He didn't mind.

Not at all.

Then, in the morning, he had Elaine again. He went to his classes curiously refreshed, happy and at peace with the world.

Tuesday he slept alone. He stayed up late working on ecology, which was getting interesting, and on invertebrate bio, which was getting difficult. And he had a little difficulty falling asleep.

I must be a man now, he thought. *I can't even fall asleep alone any more.*

Wednesday night he had dinner with Jan and went to a movie. He had been expecting to be bored stiff, but there was something strangely enjoyable about the date. It was almost as though she provided a weird reprieve from the heavy dose of sex he had been subjected to of late. At any rate, he enjoyed being with her. He liked the way she talked, the way she held his hand, the look in her eyes when she looked at him.

The movie was a dog, but that didn't seem to matter. They talked through half of it and necked through the other half. The necking was mild enough, and he wanted to laugh when he re-alized that a mild little necking session like that would have had him crawling the walls a week or two ago.

Now it was nothing.

He took her home early, explaining that he had a heavy load of classes the next day.

Which was stretching a point.

Because, after he had given the pretty little freshman a kiss good-bye and a parting squeeze of the left breast, he went to an apartment on 94th Street.

Mary Stackpole lived there.

And Mary Stackpole loved there.

Very well.

This time he played the game he would have loved to play the night of his initiation. Then he had not had time, but now he had all the time in the world.

Loads of time.

Plenty of time.

So he took as much time as he could with Mary Stackpole, playing tantalizing games with her in an effort to penetrate that icy British reserve of hers. He teased her to heights of passion, then eased off and let her squirm like a snake nailed to the earth.

He touched her and stroked her and kissed her. He took her, moving as slowly as he could, letting her passion grow while he kept his own rigidly under control.

And it worked.

Because finally she could not take it any longer, could not stand another minute or another second of what he was doing to her, and the wall of ice collapsed. No longer was she the reserved little maiden; no longer could she lie there while a man sweated and groaned on top of her.

Now she was writhing, squirming.

And screaming.

She begged him:

"Do it, Dave. Harder, harder! Oh, don't stop, please don't stop, I need it so much. Do it, do it, do it, do it, do it, do it!"

He asked her what he should do.

And she answered him, screaming a four-letter word over and over and over, screaming that word again and again until his passion rose to match hers and the word came down over their ears.

"That was mean of you," she said much later.

"Mean?"

"To tease me like that. I needed it so badly and you made me beg for it."

"But you liked it, didn't you?"

"Of course I did. I should have thought my enjoyment was obvious."

"If you liked it, what are you complaining about?"

She smiled, moving closer to him. "Who's complaining?"

"You were."

"I wasn't complaining."

"No?"

She shook her pretty head. He looked at her, at the body and the huge breasts.

"I wasn't complaining," she repeated. "I was merely saying that you were mean."

"Don't you like it?"

"Of course I do," she said. "I love mean men."

"Like me?"

"Like you."

"Then prove it to me."

He reached for her and she came to him. This time neither of them held anything back. They both put everything they had into it.

It was very good.

Very very good.

And her sigh and his sigh came at once, splitting the sky into pieces.

"See?" she said.

"Wow," he said.

"There's nothing like cooperation," she said.

Chapter 6

Friday night.

Meeting Night.

Dave met Clark Reynolds at the corner of Broadway and 115th. The English major was wearing a neat brown tweed suit with a solid brown tie. He winked broadly.

"Meeting time," he said. "Willing to bump along on the subway or should we pop for a cab?"

"I'm close to broke," Dave said. "The IRT is good enough for me. Let's roll."

On the train to Spring Street Dave asked Clark how he had come to join the Libertines. Reynolds explained that he had submitted some manuscripts to the campus literary magazine, and that Avery King was on the editorial board. King asked to see more of his work, and by accident Clark had shown him some pieces he had knocked out in his spare time.

"I hadn't meant to show them to him," Clark went on. "They were pretty strong stuff. You know, the kind of stuff a writer will do more or less for his own amusement. That kind of work never gets published, not even in the most realistic books. It's sort of like the books they have at the club quarters. Anyway, it was a lucky mistake on my part. I guess Avery must have figured that anybody who wrote stuff like that would fit perfectly into the

Libertines. Anyway, he sounded me out on it a little bit at a time, and I was interested. Hell, who wouldn't be?"

"It was about the same with me," Dave went on. "Except that I didn't know whether or not to believe Talbot. I believed him after awhile."

"Obviously."

Dave sighed. "So this is the first meeting coming up," he said. "The first real meeting, I mean. I wonder what it'll be like."

"It can't be much better than the sessions we have with the girls on our own. What more can you *do*, for God's sake?"

"I don't know," Dave said. "But I guess we'll find out."

He was right.

When they walked into the main meeting room, Avery King was on hand to welcome them. "You're early," he said. "Nobody else is here yet. I was just getting the projector set up."

"Movies?"

King nodded. "Better than usual," he said. "We're usually stuck with black-and-white. Good ones, most of the time—our supplier gives us good stuff. But this time we lucked out. Instead of a ten-minute black and white job, this is a solid hour in living color. And when I say living, I mean living."

"You've seen it?" Clark asked.

"Just the first five minutes worth. That was plenty. It's going to be a good film."

The other members began to filter in, one or two at a time, and in the interim Avery explained the procedure of movies at the Libertine meetings.

"We take our clothes off up here," he said. "The theater is downstairs in the basement. It's sound-proofed, although the movie doesn't have a sound track. Some of them do, but that's an exception and hard to come by."

"It must be."

"The basement is more than sound-proofed," King went on. "When the club took over this building, some extensive remodeling was done. The basement got a good share of it. The first thing the members did was to mat the entire floor with foam rubber four inches thick. You can see the advantages of that."

They could.

"Then they installed a screen, a stage, and a projection booth. The screen is high enough up so that you can see over people in front of you . . . even if you're lying down. The stage isn't that high, of course. But it's a raised platform, and it's also matted with foam rubber."

"For demonstrations?"

"Naturally. Now, when everybody's here, we go down to the basement naked and I roll the film. The projector's a good one—you don't have to have somebody working it. That way we all get to participate."

"Good idea."

"There are a few ground rules," Avery King went on. "You're not allowed to touch any of the girls until the movie starts. It may be a little frustrating seeing them walking around naked and not being able to grab a handful. But it's worth it. It makes everything that much more exciting once things get underway."

They nodded. King drifted off to talk to Leila Morse, and Clark buttonholed Sally Chen and began talking to her. Dave looked around, noticing that the others were beginning to undress. He saw Betty Stacey slipping out of her clothes and had an overpowering urge to run over to her and do what he had done to her that night at her apartment. The memory of that night was overwhelming and his hands began to tremble.

Instead, he forced himself to undress. He was almost completely naked when Keith Talbot walked over, nude, and handed him a glass.

"What's this?"

"Don't ask, Davey boy. Just drink up."

"But—"

"It's something that would have made your initiation a hell of a lot easier," Keith said. "A special club recipe, available only on meeting nights. A secret recipe. An aphrodisiac, you idiot. Now drink it."

The liquid was a dark purple. He tasted it. It was lukewarm, and it tasted slightly bilious. He felt like pouring it into the nearest potted palm, but he decided that what it did was more important than how it tasted. He drained the glass.

And, moments later, when he took another long look at the nude form of Betty Stacey, he saw how effective the liquid was. Every muscle in his body yearned for contact with the girl. His mouth was dry, his brain swimming in desire. He forced himself to look around, and he noticed at once that everybody in the room who was already holding an empty glass had the same desires he had.

It was fantastic.

Incredible.

Magnificent.

Silently they turned and followed Avery King out of the main room and down a darkened flight of stairs to the basement. Dave thought hysterically that they must be making a weird picture—twelve young men and women in a row, all stark naked and drugged to the brim with leaping lusts.

Ahead of him Leila Morse walked. If there was one girl he shouldn't have to walk behind in his present condition, it was Leila Morse. Her magnificent bottom twitched and wiggled, and it was all he could do to keep from reaching out with both hands and drawing her close to him. He wanted to run his hands over her, wanted to take her then and there.

But he remembered the rules.

No fun games until the movie began.

Behind him, he discovered without turning around, walked Mary Stackpole. He found this out when he stopped short at one point and her big breasts bumped into him. While he didn't recognize the contact of her breasts specifically—he knew it was Mary because she was considerably taller than the rest of the girls, and her breasts bumped him higher up than anyone else's would have.

Leila Morse in front.

Mary Stackpole behind.

It was enough to make him go out of his skull and run screaming in all directions. Especially with the aphrodisiac bubbling through his veins, intoxicating him and working him up to fever pitch. It was hard, but he managed to bring himself under control, managed to hold back the wild impulses that coursed through him.

Then they were in the basement.

It was almost completely dark. Only the screen was illuminated, casting an eerie glow over the stage below it. He bumped into a girl, excused himself and sat down on the soft well-padded floor, his nerves on edge and his eyes on the screen.

The room was silent. Absolutely silent.

Then the movie began.

TITLE CARD: PASSIONATE YEARNINGS

The camera pans a one-room apartment. A battered dresser stands in one corner of the room, its top scarred with the burns of forgotten cigarettes. A chair near the dresser is piled high with discarded clothing. One corner of the single room serves as the kitchen, complete with a four-burner hot-plate resting on top of a small refrigerator. The camera turns its attention to each of these objects. Then it moves for a long shot of the bed and dollies in for a close-up.

A woman is lying on the bed, her body covered only by a single sheet. Her long blonde hair is spread out over a pillow, and her eyes are closed. She tosses around, giving the impression of a restless sort of slumber. The motion accents the contour of her body beneath the sheet.

Shot of an alarm clock on the dresser.

SUBTITLE: "RING-A-LING-A-LING."

In response to the alarm, the woman yawns powerfully, throws off the sheet and strides across the room to the dresser. The camera follows her from the side. She is wearing a sheer silk nightgown, and the camera manages to catch slight glimpses of the body beneath the nightgown. The nightgown is pink.

Shot of hand shutting off alarm.

Close-up of woman's face as she yawns once more. She is wearing both lipstick and mascara, which seems unusual. But it does look good on her. She is a very attractive woman, with strong Nordic features and very white teeth.

Medium shot of woman. Now she yawns with her whole body, stretching her arms out so that the nightgown falls open. Her breasts are visible now. They are quite large, with the slight sag evident in the body of a mature woman.

Slowly the camera dollies in for a shot of the breasts. The woman cups them in her hands—her nails glow with scarlet nail-polish—and alternately raises and lowers them.

The woman shrugs and the pink nightgown falls to the floor. Now, very slowly, the camera pans her body. It moves downward from her breasts, past her stomach to her hips. Her thighs are clutched tight together. Her legs are very long and quite shapely.

SUBTITLE: "WHAT A BEAUTIFUL MORNING."

The woman turns and walks back to the bed. The camera follows her from the rear, focusing on her posterior. Her hips sway insinuatingly as she walks.

Now the woman is sitting on the edge of the bed. Her thighs are clenched together, and the camera moves in for an extreme close-up of them.

Slowly she opens them.

SUBTITLE: "THIS IS MY—"

The camera moves back and forth over the area under investigation. For several seconds the woman sits passively. Then her fingers stray to the area now examined. They touch and probe the area and the camera follows her activity with cinematographic interest. Her fingers are busy.

Long shot of the woman sitting on the edge of the bed. She sighs, yawns again, and begins to touch herself once more.

SUBTITLE: "I'M SO HOT I CAN'T STAND IT."

The woman stands up, still naked, and crosses the room again, this time to the kitchen area. She goes to the refrigerator and opens it.

The camera contemplates the contents of the refrigerator. The food is a strange assortment. In turn the camera focuses upon a midget salami, a carrot, and a frankfurter.

Then the camera discovers a banana. Apparently the woman has ignored United Fruit's injunction against keeping bananas in the refrigerator. At any rate, she picks up the banana, closes the refrigerator, and returns to the edge of the bed.

SUBTITLE: "JUST WHAT I NEED."

The woman peels the banana, dropping the skin to the floor. Then she puts the banana to a use which United Fruit probably never believed possible. The camera examines this activity from every conceivable angle. It dips back for shots of the woman's face contorted in an expression of passion.

SUBTITLE: "THIS IS GREAT!"

More play with the banana.

SUBTITLE: "I'M STARVING!"

The woman retrieves the banana, contemplates it carefully, and devours it.

Then, in turn, she does the same with the carrot, the frankfurter, and, finally the midget salami.

The moment the movie started, Dave Forrester felt warm female flesh rub up against him. His hands went to the girl, coursing over her body. He took her breasts in his warm hands and squeezed so hard that the girl gave a little yelp of pain.

They sat side by side. And, with eager hands, they began to explore each other's body.

The girl was Sandy Wilkins.

They went on touching, and all the while their eyes were riveted to the screen. Dave had never seen anything like the movie in his life. He had seen still shots, but never movies. And this movie, in color, was so lifelike it was incredible. Watching it was like being in the same room.

It was great.

Wonderful.

But it posed a problem.

"I want you," he whispered into Sandy's ear.

"I want you, too."

"But . . . you're going to think this is pretty silly. I guess it is."

"What?"

"I . . . don't want to stop looking at the movie. I never saw anything like it before."

"I understand."

He cupped her breast. He longed to fall upon her, to seek possession of her and take her viciously and completely.

But he couldn't tear his eyes off the screen.

"Could we do it so that I can watch the movie?"

Sandy giggled. "You're awfully selfish," she said.

"What do you mean?"

"I mean I want to watch the movie myself. After all it's only fair."

"Then what do we do?"

The girl giggled again. "Did you ever own a dog?"

"Once. A cocker spaniel. Why?"

"The dogs know the answer."

"Oh."

"Now do you understand?"

He understood perfectly.

It began.

And, while he made violent love to the warm, twitching girl before him, his eyes were riveted to the screen.

The woman has finished her autoerotic routine. This is fortunate, for now the refrigerator is empty. The blonde woman sits on the edge of the bed as before, idly massaging her breasts with her hands. She seems bored.

Subtitle: "Oh, I am so lonely."

She gets up and begins to pace the floor, back and forth, to and fro. It is a rather odd sight—a tall, lovely blonde, walking back and forth with her behind swaying and her breasts bobbing.

Close-up of her face.

Subtitle: "I wish somebody would come to see me."

Long shot of the door to the apartment.

Subtitle: "Knock, knock, knock."

Shot of woman's face, smiling.

Shot of woman putting on pink nightgown once again.

Another shot of woman s face.

Subtitle: "Come in."

The door opens. Another woman enters, this one younger and shorter. She is a brunette, with very short and very dark brown hair.

She looks Latin, either Spanish or Italian. Her complexion is quite dark.

   Shot of brunette's face.

   SUBTITLE: "COULD I BORROW A CUP OF SUGAR?"

   Shot of blonde's face.

   SUBTITLE: "I HAVE NO SUGAR BUT STAY ANYWAY."

   The blonde crosses the room and takes a long look at the brunette.

   Obligingly the camera pans the brunette's body, starting with her face. She is wearing a jet black blouse that buttons down the front, a black skirt, and black sandals. She is slender, but her breasts seem to be well-formed, as well as one can tell through the black blouse.

   The blonde moves closer to the brunette, placing her hands on the dark girl's shoulders.

   SUBTITLE: "YOU'RE NICE."

   Smiling widely, the blonde removes her pink nightgown.

   Close-up of the brunette's face. She is smiling, her eyes wide.

   Shot of the blonde, showing off her body. She touches her breasts, her belly, her thighs. Then she smiles still more happily.

   SUBTITLE: "NOW I WANT TO SEE YOU."

   The blonde begins to undress the brunette. She unbuttons the dark girl's blouse and thrusts a hand inside. Then she removes the blouse completely and begins to squeeze the brunette's small but nice breasts.

   The brunette reciprocates, reaching for the blonde's large breasts and squeezing them with both hands.

   SUBTITLE: "NOW I WANT TO LOOK AT YOUR—"

   The blonde removes the brunette's skirt and sandals. She steps back and the camera makes a thorough study of the brunette's charms. Breasts, arms, legs, posterior—all the separate components which comprise the brunette are carefully inventoried by the searching eye of the camera.

SUBTITLE: "DO YOU WANT TO—ME?"

Shot of brunette, nodding in very definite agreement with the suggestion.

The blonde walks over to the bed and stretches out on her back. The brunette follows her and sits on the edge of the bed, looking down at her.

They kiss.

The camera investigates the kiss thoroughly. It focuses first on their mouths locked in combat. Then it moves down, discovering that the small firm breasts of the brunette are pressed tight against the full breasts of the blonde. The brunette raises herself slightly on her elbows and brushes her breasts back and forth so that her nipples rub against the nipples of the blonde.

Then the camera moves lower still. The girls are pressed together all the way, and their bodies are churning gently.

The kiss lasts a long time.

Then the brunette sits up again, very happy, and the camera focuses on the blonde's face.

SUBTITLE: "NOW GIVE ME A GOOD—"

The brunette does just that. She begins by kissing the blonde's breast.

She moves lower.

The camera plays the field. First it focuses on the brunette's mouth, examining the clever movements of lips and tongue. Then it returns to the blonde's face, which is animated in an expression of supreme joy.

SUBTITLE: "—IT AS HARD AS YOU CAN!"
And the brunette girl did just as she was told.

Avery King was making love to Elaine Rice. Their bodies flexed and strained together. Elaine moaned again and again.

Near them, Sally Chen sat listening to them and watching the two women on the screen.

Simply saying that Sally Chen had never seen two women make love before would be gravely understating the case. The lovely, dainty Chinese girl had been a virgin during her freshman year at the college. For most of it, that is. Then she had been skillfully seduced by her steady date.

The boy had left her once his mission was accomplished. From then on, Sally Chen adopted a simple form of morality. If she liked a boy, she slept with him. It was that simple.

But now she was watching two women make love. This was not simple at all. It was something she had thought of before, but something she had never done. She had never considered it too seriously—but now, watching the things the blonde woman was experiencing from the brunette woman, long dormant desires began to burn within her lovely body.

Elaine moaned again.

Sally remembered what Elaine had looked like without clothes on. In her mind, Sally became the brunette on the screen.

Elaine became the blonde.

And Elaine moaned again.

And again.

And again . . .

And it was over. Sally listened intently as Avery King rolled away from Elaine.

Now it was her turn. Her turn . . .

Slowly she made her way over to Elaine's side. She reached out a hand and touched Elaine. It was, she discovered, very nice to touch another woman. Different from touching a man. Elaine's skin was very soft, very smooth. She ran her hand over Elaine and felt herself tremble.

"God," said Elaine. "Another one!"

Elaine reached out a hand.

"Don't tell me who it is," she said. "I've had everybody here. All I have to do is touch and I'll find out."

Sally sat, trembling, as Elaine's hand found her thigh and began to course upward. Her skin was alive, vibrant, under Elaine's soft hand.

Elaine's hand reached its destination.

Elaine's hand did not find what it was looking for.

"God," Elaine said. "You're a girl!"

"Why not? You saw the movie, Elaine. You saw what it's like. Why don't we do it?"

Elaine hesitated. "But—"

"It looks like fun," Sally said. "It looks like lots of fun. What do we have to lose by trying it?"

"I don't know—"

"Please!"

"Well, maybe. Which do you want to do? I mean, do you want to play the part of the blonde or the brunette?"

"The brunette."

"I guess that would be okay. I mean, I wouldn't have to *do* any-thing, would I?"

"Nothing," Sally said. "All you have to do is lie still and let me love you."

"It just seems . . . sick."

"Sick?"

"You know. Perverted."

Sally laughed, a low, tinkling laugh.

"What's so funny?"

"You lily-of-the-valley," Sally said. "You healthy, normal girl. We're all sick, Elaine. If we weren't sick we wouldn't be here! This is a sick and perverted club and we belong to it because we're sick and perverted people. Now will you let me do it to you or not?"

"All right."

Elaine lay back on the padded floor. And Sally crouched over her, taking her cues from the images on the screen, doing every-thing to Elaine that the brunette had done to the blonde.

She liked it.

She liked it very much.

And so did Elaine.

The blonde and the brunette have absolutely exhausted the rep-ertoire of lesbian practices. They lie back, exhausted, in the position of their last game. The blonde's head is at the foot of the bed. The brunette's head is at the head of the bed.

Long shot of the door.

SUBTITLE: "KNOCK, KNOCK, KNOCK."

Shot of the blonde and brunette. They are startled at the inter-ruption. The brunette jumps up, sweeps up her clothing in her arms and darts into the closet. She squeezes inside and closes the door after her.

Shot of the blonde, getting up from the bed.

SUBTITLE: "JUST A MINUTE."

The blonde scoops up her nightgown and puts it on once more. She walks to the door and opens it. The boy standing there is about fifteen years old. He has a newsboy's changemaker on his belt and is carrying a little record book in his hand.

SUBTITLE: "YOU OWE ME A DOLLAR FOR THE COURIER."

The blonde beckons the boy inside. Then she motions him to stay where he is while she hurries to the closet. She opens the door about an inch.

SUBTITLE: "NOW WE CAN HAVE SOME MORE FUN."

The blonde walks back to the newsboy. He is staring at her, and the camera shows his expression. Medium shot of the woman, removing her nightgown.

Shot of the boy's face.

SUBTITLE: "WOULD YOU LIKE TO—ME, LITTLE BOY?"

Shot of the boy. He is obviously terrified. He turns to go, but the blonde wraps her arms around his waist and holds onto him securely.

SUBTITLE: "COME OUT OF THE CLOSET AND HELP ME."

The brunette comes out of the closet and hurries over to where the blonde is holding the newsboy captive. She walks around in front of the newsboy and gives him—and the camera as well—a good look at her naked body.

Then she begins to undress him.

The newsboy struggles, but he is powerless. The blonde holds him from behind and the brunette divests him of his shirt, his pants, his shoes, his socks, his underwear.

SUBTITLE: "WE'LL HAVE FUN WITH HIM."

The brunette commences to explore the boy's body with eager fingers. The blonde joins in the fun, and the two of them tease the boy mercilessly.

SUBTITLE: "LET'S TAKE HIM TO BED."

Together, the blonde and the brunette lead the unwilling boy to the bed. They force him to lie on his back, and the blonde sits on his chest so that he cannot move.

Then the brunette begins to do things to him.

Close-up.

The camera studies the work of the brunette's hands.

The boy does not respond.

SUBTITLE: "HE'S A BAD BOY. LET'S GIVE HIM A SPANKING."

Together, the two women roll the boy over. They make him lie on his stomach with his head in the brunette's lap. Then the blonde begins to slap him across the posterior with her open palm. The brunette joins in.

Shot of the boy's face, contorted in pain.

SUBTITLE: "OWWWWW! THAT HURTS!"

They continue to slap him.

SUBTITLE: "I'LL DO ANYTHING. JUST STOP THAT!"

Shot of the brunette, smiling.

Shot of the blonde smiling.

They roll the boy over onto his back again. Now the blonde begins kissing him upon the mouth, her tongue probing far between his lips. The camera closes in on their kiss.

The kiss ends. The blonde grins hugely, then places one of her large breasts to the boy's mouth.

Subtitle: "Kiss it."

The boy does as he is told, and the camera comes in for an extreme close-up of his mouth and her breast. Then the camera pans slowly, very slowly, over the boy's body. Once again the brunette is manipulating the boy skillfully, and this time she is getting the desired reaction.

The brunette seats herself astride the boy.

Close-up to the area's involved.

The brunette forces the boy to make love to her in that position, while the blonde keeps her breast to his mouth. The camera examines the three-way effort from all angles until it is over.

Then the boy makes love to the blonde, while the brunette does something else to the boy. They continue in a variety of acts until all three are properly exhausted. By now the boy has been converted to the sport and is a more than willing participant in all activity.

Final shot: The boy kneels on the bed. The blonde kneels on one side of him, the brunette on the other. He has an arm around each, with one hand on one of the blonde's large breasts and the other on one of the small breasts of the dark girl.

Subtitle: "This is true love."

Title card: THE END

Hardly anyone realized that the movie was over.

The padded floor of the movie room was the scene of an orgy more complex than any in the history of the world since the fall of the Roman Empire. The entire floor was covered with couples, seemingly inexhaustible as a result of the drug they had all imbibed. The couples made love with incredible skill, incredible ingenuity, and incredible speed.

Dave Forrester was temporarily alone. After a seemingly endless parade of women, interspersed with views of the perversion transpiring upon the silver screen, he had managed to haul himself off to a corner.

He was tired.

And sick.

Now that the movie was over, a dull blue light suffused the room. It was very dim, but it was enough for him to see by. He looked around the room, looked at the couples. Everybody seemed to be busy, and this baffled him for a moment. After all, he was out of the picture. Shouldn't there be one girl left over?

And then that problem was solved. He saw Betty Stacey and Leila Morse, both of them making love to Marty Pekorsky. Evidently they had been inspired by the movie.

He looked at them and felt sick.

Before, this would have been exciting. Now he was just past the point of excitement. All he could think of was how sick, how disgusting the entire spectacle was to his eyes. Maybe, he thought, he had reached the saturation point. Maybe he had had so much sex at once that the mere thought of sex was enough to make him want to vomit.

But that wasn't it. Because sex itself still seemed to him to be something lovely, something beautiful. Sex between a married couple, or sex between a couple really in love. Or, for that matter, the sort of relationship he had had with Sheila Reeves at camp that summer, where friendship and honest physical attraction had been the factors that had brought them together.

That was still all right in his eyes.

But *this!*

He shook his head. The frightening picture before him of couples copulating madly, barely knowing who they were doing it to, was too much for him. This wasn't love. It wasn't even decent sex.

It was perversion.

For the first time he began to see the Libertines in their true light. At first, when any experience had been desirable, when he had craved sexual contact like a thirsty man craves water, the Libertines were the answer to his wildest dreams.

Now it was different.

A thirsty man doesn't stop to see whether water offered to him is poisoned. A man hungry for sexual experience doesn't stop to see whether the experience is evil, poisonous.

He had not stopped.

And now he was enmeshed in corruption.

He looked at Keith Talbot, a boy who had been his . . . well, his idol. Now it sickened him to look at Talbot. Keith was rolling around on the floor with a woman, doing something that two of the lesbians had done on the screen.

It was sickening.

Disgusting.

Perverted.

Slowly he hoisted himself to his feet, knowing that he had to leave before he threw up all over a roomful of intertwined couples. He reached the door, opened it, and got out of the room. Nobody saw him go—all of them were too busy with their own sexual peccadilloes. He closed the door behind him and scrambled up the basement staircase in total darkness.

He found the main room and managed to locate his own clothing. He dressed in a hurry, not bothering to put on his socks. Instead he stuffed them into his pockets. Then, reeling, he dashed for the door and headed out into the night.

He was weak in the knees and had to lean against a building for support. Then the memory of the whole spectacle surged once more through his burning brain and his stomach turned over. He was sick, thoroughly sick, emptying his stomach onto the pavement of Spring Street.

He staggered away blindly, wanting only to escape. He rushed onward, finally reaching a wide street where there was enough traffic to justify an occasional cruising cab. He managed to hail a cab and sank into the back seat. All he wanted was solitude, peace, quiet. He was through with the Libertines forever.

CHAPTER 7

His resolution was just as strong Saturday as it had been Friday night. As far as he was concerned, the Libertines didn't exist. He simply wasn't interested in them. If they wanted to pick him for his dues, well, that was all right. He didn't care about the money. The important thing, as far as he was concerned, was to avoid any contact with the male and female members of the organization. If he got hard up he would go up to Harlem and buy himself a woman. That was cleaner and more decent than participating in their revolting orgies.

Hell, he *had* a girl. He was dating Jan Chatterton that night, and he would continue to date her. She was a sweet, decent girl, nicer than any of them and just as pretty. She didn't possess the striking beauty of Betty Stacey, but she was as attractive as any of the others and more attractive than most.

He would go right on dating her, maybe three times a week instead of two, and he would concentrate on having a good time instead of trying to eradicate her virginity. If their relationship developed to the point where they both wanted to sleep together, well, that was something he'd be all in favor of. But he wasn't going to push anything. He'd had enough of loveless, thoughtless sex in the short time he'd been in the Libertines. He didn't want any more of that.

He showered half a dozen times Saturday morning, trying to wash the stench of the night before out of his system. That afternoon he loaded himself with schoolwork, studying for two hours in the library and three more hours in his room. He was happy to discover that the academic work drove other thoughts from his mind. It accomplished two things at once, making the day pass more quickly and getting a load of work out of the way.

The second point was at least as important as the first. During the past week, what with all the time he'd been spending in bed with various girls, he hadn't put in a hell of a lot of time at his books. He'd attended most of his classes, but he had passed up a lot of required reading and had gotten behind in several courses. It was nothing that he couldn't make up almost at once, but it drove home a lesson to him.

From now on, he decided, he wouldn't get behind at all. He'd hit the books regularly, and hard and between studying and Jan he'd be too busy to worry about the Libertines. That was the best answer to his problems.

He ate dinner alone, a quick and tasteless meal at the cafeteria. Then he called Jan. First, as usual, he went through the ritual of asking a hall-mate to call her. Then her voice came over the wire and he realized how much he liked her.

"Can you be ready by 7:30?"

"That's a whole hour from now," she said. "I never have that much time to get ready when I go out with you. Is something the matter?"

He laughed. "Just wanted you to get extra pretty."

"Something special?"

"Not exactly."

"Where are we going?"

"A jazz club," he said.

"Really?"

"Unless you hate jazz, or something."

"I *love* jazz," she said. "And I'd *love* to go. Is it one of those nasty nests of perversion where everybody smokes marijuana and walks along the ceiling?"

"You've been reading too many comic books," he told her. "It's not like that at all. People drink beer and sit very quietly and listen to the music."

"Wonderful."

"7:30?"

"Wonderful."

"Well, I'll see you then."

"Wonderful," she said a third time.

"Is it really?"

"Really what?"

"Really wonderful."

"It really is," she said. "And so are you."

She rang off, leaving him standing there with a phone in his hand and a silly grin spreading slowly on his face. After a few minutes of grinning he managed to hang up the receiver and walk to his room to get dressed for the date.

He stared at her.

"Is something wrong, Dave? Do I have my head on backwards or am I wearing blue lipstick or what?"

"The dress," he said.

"Don't you like it?"

"It's lovely," he said. "I've never seen anything like it. It looks great on you."

"Thanks," she said.

"I mean it."

"Thanks a lot."

"Did I say something wrong?"

"I wore this dress on our first date."

"Oh," he said hollowly.

"I can see I made quite an impression on you."

"Uh—"

"But I'm glad you like it. This time, anyway."

"Ulp—"

"Let's go," she said. "You look awfully sad. Pull yourself together. How do we get to this place?"

"Subway is easiest," he said. "Except you might get your dress messed up. Maybe we better take a cab."

"This dress is four years old," she said. "So let's take the subway before I rip off my lovely dress and strangle you with it. If I did that, people would probably stop and stare at me, and that wouldn't be too good, would it? So let's go."

The Dime Note, a small and relatively unknown establishment devoted to progressive jazz, was located on a quiet corner in Chelsea. The three other establishments at the corner of Eighth Avenue and 25th Street were: a cigar store serving as a numbers drop and a bookmaking establishment, a Spanish-speaking bar where hustlers waited for phone calls, and a Greek coffeehouse where old men sipped cups of thick black coffee and peddled hashish. On such a corner, the police were a natural phenomenon.

They would come from time to time, passing the cigar store, the cafe, and the cathouse, and would descend upon the proprietor of the Dime Note, suspending his license for serving an occasional beer to an occasional minor. Since the cigar store, the cafe and the cathouse all contributed greatly and frequently to everybody from the captain to the cop on the beat, and since the proprietor of the Dime Note did not, this was the usual order of business.

Dave and Jan arrived a few minutes after eight. The first set was just getting under way, and they went quickly to a table near the front and ordered a pair of beers. Then they began to pay attention to the music.

A quartet was on stage—piano, bass, drums, and tenor saxophone. They were a relatively new group, and although Dave had heard the piano player and the bass player on occasional records, the tenor man and the drummer were new to him. He listened carefully and he liked what he heard.

Then tenor was gutsy, merging the funkiness of the blues with the complexities of bop and grinding the result out with force, verve, and power. The drummer used the top cymbal and stayed on top of the beat, kicking the group along. The piano player, who didn't take one solo during the entire first set, laid down a base of chords that provided a perfect groundwork for the tenor's improvisations. The bass was solid, increasing the dimension of the group, building on the chord structure, holding the rhythm.

They listened to the first three numbers without saying a word. The beer arrived and they poured, clinked glasses, and drank. And went on listening.

The set ended. The musicians stepped down, found their table, and ordered fresh drinks. Somebody somewhere dropped a dime in a jukebox and played a Miles Davis record. Dave looked at Jan, and she smiled.

"It's easy to get lost," she said. "The music has so much happening in it. I completely forgot where I was and everything. There was just me and the music."

"I know what you mean."

"It's good we've gone out before," she said. "It wouldn't have made much of an impression if this were our first date. You know, just getting lost and not saying a word to you. You don't mind, do you?"

"Of course not. I was a little worried that you might mind if I ignored you."

She grinned. "I have a confession to make."

"Make it."

"I told you I loved jazz. It was a lie."

"You hate it?"

"I love it."

"You just said—"

"I never listened to it before. Oh, an occasional record that I half heard. But I never went to a club like this before."

"Really?"

"Really."

"Are you glad you came?"

"Very glad."

"Then so am I."

He reached across the table and his hand found her hand. He looked into her eyes and was very glad that he had found her. He tried to imagine himself out on a date with one of the girls who belonged to the Libertines. It was impossible. Some of them might well be nice girls underneath it all, but sex was so predominant in any relationship they formed that all other qualities rapidly became nonexistent.

He couldn't possibly have taken Leila Morse or Elaine Rice to the Dime Note. It was out of the question. If he had had a "date" with one of those girls, they would have gone directly to bed. That, in their eyes, was the beginning and ending of the Universe. Anything else was nothing but wrapping paper, formality to be dispensed with whenever possible.

If they could see him now, he thought, they would think he was pretty much of a cornball. Well, to hell with them. He was listening to good music and spending time in the company of a sweet and pleasant girl.

Maybe it was square to prefer something like that to meaningless, mindless sex. If so, well, he was square. And damned proud to be square.

The break ended. The musicians stood up one at a time and found their way back to the stand. They picked up or sat down at their instruments, tuned up, got ready to play.

He sat back in his chair. He sipped at his beer and prepared to listen to more music.

He did not let go of her hand.

They stayed at the Dime Note until almost midnight. Then he asked her if she was hungry, and she said that she could stand to stop for a bite if he wanted to, and he said that frankly he was starving and they ought to find a good place to eat.

This time they took a cab instead of a subway. He gave the taxi driver the address of a German tavern on the East Side where they had hot roast beef sandwiches on kummelweck rolls and steins of cold ale.

"Wonderful," she said.

"The food?"

"Uh-huh. And the ale."

"Is that all?"

"And you," she said. "But I already told you that you were wonderful. You ought to know it by now."

He wondered why he felt foolish.

They took another cab when they left the restaurant, at which time she told him he was spending far too much money on her and he agreed that he probably was but that she was worth it. In the cab she came to him with her little mouth ready to be kissed. He kissed her, held her very close, and felt very good.

They kissed all the way home. He knew that he could touch her breasts if he wanted to, could run his hand up her thigh beneath her dress. But he knew also that he did not want to do anything to cheapen what they had. It was too good, too valuable, and he did not want to ruin it.

He paid off the cab, took her hand in his, and they walked without saying a word directly to the bench where they had sat before. They sat down and looked at each other, and then they kissed. It was a full kiss, with her mouth opening at once to his, her tongue plunging deep into his mouth, her body taut and warm against him.

"Dave—"

"I know," he said.

"It's so nice."

"I know."

They kissed again.

"I wish we had some place to be alone," she said. "That's what I wish. I wish we could go somewhere and close a door and keep the rest of the world away."

"I know."

"All by ourselves," she said. "All alone."

For a quick moment he thought of the apartment where he and Clark were "living." He ought to be able to get *some* use out of it, he thought savagely. But he rejected the thought at once. He couldn't bring a girl like Jan to a place like that. It was ironic—the one girl he wanted to be alone with, and he couldn't use the place he'd rented for the specific purpose of being alone with girls. It was a pain in the neck.

"Kiss me," she said.

He kissed her. Then, in the middle of the kiss, she took his hand and placed it upon her breast. He held her, not pinching, not squeezing, merely held her very tenderly. And the passion that went through them both at once was true passion, not sexual fever. He wanted her—not any woman, but her. And he knew that she felt the same way about him.

They remained on the bench for half an hour. They talked, they kissed, and he touched her sleeping breasts and felt them awaken to him.

It was good.

Then he took her back to her dormitory, where he kissed her again and touched her again and, finally, said good-bye to her.

Then he walked off to his own dormitory and to sleep.

• • •

Sunday was calm. He studied, listened to music, read a paperback novel. He met Jan at the cafe for dinner, talked to her for a half hour, then went back and hit the books for a little while before hitting the sack.

That was Sunday.

Monday the bomb fell.

It happened Monday evening. He was sitting in his room, poring over the ecology text and trying to make some sense out of a thoroughly incomprehensible passage, when a face appeared briefly in the doorway and told him that the phone was for him. He closed the book gently and went to the phone.

It was Betty Stacey.

"I was wondering where you've been," she said. "Nobody's seen you since the meeting. I asked around and it's as if you disappeared."

"I've been busy," he said.

"Busy?"

"Studying."

"The midnight oil," she said. "Well, enough of that. Come on over, why don't you?"

"I can't."

"You can't?"

"Not tonight."

"Why not?"

He told her he had to study.

"Just for a little while," she coaxed. "I won't keep you long. And I'm very lonely."

He took a deep breath, then let it all out at once. "I'm quitting," he said. "Quitting the . . . club. I'm through with it, Betty. And I'm not coming over."

There was a long and ominous pause.

Then: "You'd better come over here right away."

"I told you—"

"I don't give a damn what you told me," she snapped. "Get over here in one hell of a hurry. I've got something to tell you, sweetie pie, and I don't want to tell you over the phone. So shake the lead out of your butt and move it!"

She hung up.

He stood for a moment, not sure what he ought to do next. Then he put the receiver where it belonged and began to move. He left the dorm without returning to his room, headed straight across campus to Broadway and down the street toward her apartment. He was almost running.

She did not seem glad to see him.

"So you're quitting," she said. "Little Boy Blue got fed up. Now he's going to pick up his marbles and go home. It that the way it goes?"

"More or less."

"Mind telling me why?"

He told her as well as he could. He told her it was sickening and disgusting and wrong. He told her that he didn't need any longer the cheap outlet that the club provided. He told her he was leading a decent life and going with a decent girl, and that he wanted to preserve no ties with her or with any other member of the Libertines. He told her he was through, through permanently and forever, through with the whole stinking mess.

That is what he told her.

Then she told him.

"You silly son of a bitch," she said. "You think this is some Lions Club you join and quit when you damn well feel like it? You're wrong, buddy boy. Dead wrong."

"I didn't sign anything. If I want to quit—"

"—it's too damned bad," she finished for him. "Nobody leaves the Libertines."

"You don't have to worry," he told her. "I wouldn't tell anybody anything, nothing like that. I just want to get out. That's all. I want to get out. The club won't miss me. I'm just an ordinary guy. I can be replaced without any trouble to anybody. I'll forget you and you forget me. That's all there is to it."

"You think so?"

"Of course."

"You're wrong."

He shifted nervously from one foot to the other. He had expected some sort of argument, but being told flatly that he had to stay in was something he had been thoroughly unprepared for. He decided that she must be bluffing. How could she keep him in against his will?

It was ridiculous.

"You think you can walk right out?"

"Sure. Why not?"

"Wait here a minute," she told him. "And I'll show you why not, you damned little idiot."

He waited, stung by her words, while she disappeared. She reappeared carrying a picture. At first he thought it was the one she had shown him before he had made love to her for the first time.

Then he took a good look.

It was similar, all right. Except that the face in the picture, the face planting nauseating kisses between Betty Stacey's plump thighs, was a face he recognized too well.

It was *his* face.

"How . . . how did you get this?"

"With a hidden camera and a remote shutter switch," she said, evidently quite proud of herself. "I like to have pictures of myself with men. This time one of them came in handy."

He tore the picture in half, then tore the halves in half again.

"Fool," she said. "That's a print. I have the negative. One picture for your parents, one for your sweet and decent girl friend, maybe one for the school authorities. One for every prospective employer you ever have for the rest of your life. One for this and one for that. You might have a tough time getting married, Dave. Or getting a degree or a job or anything else in this world. Would you like everybody to see this picture?"

"You bitch!"

She laughed in his face. "You fool! You think you're the first person to ever want to quit the Libertines? *I* wanted to, you idiot. Why do you think they have the initiation? It's filmed, you fool. The club has the film on file. This picture is just a sample."

His heart fell.

"So you won't quit," she said. "If you want to pass up sex, that's your business. I tried that for a month. I had to go if a boy called me, just as you have to come running when a girl calls you. But I passed up as many opportunities for it as I could. Then I realized that I couldn't get out and I might as well make the most of it.

You'll realize that one of these days. But you won't quit. No matter what you do, you won't quit."

"What—"

"You'll come when you're called," she said. "And you'll go to every meeting. Some of the girls you can tell that you're busy. You better not try that excuse on me, though. I know better. When I want you, you come on the run. You don't even stop to dress, not if you know what's good for you. Got that?"

He nodded, broken.

"Unhappy?"

He looked away.

"Come on," she said. "Tell me your problems. I'm your queen, remember? You can tell me all about it. What's on your little mind, honey?"

"Nothing."

"Fine," she said. "Fine."

He was sick and he was afraid he was going to have to throw up. He didn't know what he could do. If his parents or Jan ever saw that filthy picture, then it was all over. He could throw up his books and go home, or join the foreign legion, or something like that. Whatever way he looked at it, he was stuck. There was no way out. He would have to do what she said.

Go to the foul meetings.

Sleep with the girls when they asked for it.

Be a Libertine.

A Libertine.

A Libertine ...

His knees went weak. He turned away from her, heading for

the door, knowing that he simply had to get away and be by himself and think.

"Where are you going?"

"Out."

"That's what you think. Come over here."

He hesitated. Then he knew that he could not leave her until she told him to leave, could in fact do nothing in the world without her permission. He felt like a slave.

"You go when I tell you to go. Now you stay. I'm not through with you."

"What do you want from me?"

"Sex."

She made it sound dirty.

"How?"

"You know how."

And he knew.

He stood there, broken and half-dead while she took off her clothes. He looked at her body and he wondered how he could ever have found it desirable. The beauty was there, all right, but it was sick and twisted beauty, the face and body of an angel surrounding the soul of a devil, a soul straight from hell. He looked at her and hated her.

"Strip."

"Kneel."

He knelt before her.

"Now be obedient to your queen."

And, sick and disgusted though he was, he began to do what she wanted him to do. He tried to hurry the job but, sadistically, she made him do everything he had done the first time. He kissed her toes. He kissed the soles of her feet, her insteps, her ankles. He kissed her legs, making his way very slowly up her calves to her knees.

Higher.

Higher.

Higher.

"My slave," she was saying. "My little slave. My little boy. The queen's little boy. Kiss me silly, little boy. Kiss me till I can't stand it any more. Kiss me and drive me wild!"

He did what she said. His mouth crept higher along the inside of her thigh, just as it had done before. But now there was a difference. Now he was an unwilling participant. Before everything he had done to her had excited him.

Now it sickened him.

Higher.

Higher.

Higher.

"Now do it," she said. "Do it, slave. Do it to your queen. Kiss it and drive your queen positively ecstatic. Make it good for your queen, slave."

He began to do what she wanted him to do.

Slowly, at first.

Then faster.

Faster.

Faster . . .

And something strange began to happen for him. Although he was disgusted, sick of her and sick with himself, although he hated her and hated himself and hated above all what he was forced to do to her, it began to happen.

He began to get excited.

"You like it, don't you, slave? You love it just as much as I do. You hate yourself, but you love what you're doing. Don't you, slave? Don't you love it?"

On.

And on.

And on.

Stronger.

And stronger.

And stronger.

Deeper.

And constantly more exciting, with the passion building persistently within him no matter how desperately he struggled against it. He felt her reaching and straining for fulfillment and her passion communicated itself to him at once. He needed her now, needed her desperately, and loved and hated her all at once, loved her from the depth of his need and hated her from the very depth of his being.

It began to happen to her.

To her and for her.

And, with a giant shudder, she strained to the very peak of passion and was through.

He was not.

He stood up, his eyes wild, and he moved toward her. His arms held her and he forced her down on the rug, down onto the floor.

She began to laugh at him.

And he took her, took her in greed and pain and desperation, took her with lust in his blood and hate in his heart, while the searing sound of her shrill discordant laughter rang in his ears.

CHAPTER 8

It was bad . . .

His head reeled and his heart jumped back and forth, sick. He had been a traitor to himself. He had obeyed Betty because there was no way to avoid it, and then he had committed the unforgiveable sin of responding completely to her.

Bad.

Very bad.

He had left her now, left her after throwing her down upon the floor and making sick, horrible love to her. And now he was walking back to his dormitory.

It was drizzling—a light rain that made up in persistence what it lacked in power. But he barely noticed the rain, barely remembered not to step in puddles of water.

He had other things to worry about.

He stopped at a bar at the corner of 95th and Broadway and ordered a beer. There was a woman behind the bar, not much more than a girl, really. She set the bottle of beer before him with a flourish and gave him a smile that told him quite plainly that she could be had. He looked at her—her hair, a little darker than blonde, was drawn back into a severe bun. Her apron was too tight, and her breasts too big for it. She was not pretty in any sense of the word, but she was incredibly sensual. She was a woman quite literally built to be banged.

He was not interested.

He poured beer against the side of a frosted glass. He sipped the beer and tried to think straight.

It had been so simple. First, he had joined the Libertines. He had gotten a certain amount of enjoyment out of his association with the club, and then, when he had obtained a clear and accurate picture of the organization and of himself, he had realized that it was not for him.

So he had quit.

At least, that was the way he had thought it was going to go. But evidently, that was not how it was going to work out. The first thing to consider, of course, was the fact that they were not letting him go. He remembered the picture Betty had showed him and shuddered involuntarily. And, if what she told him was true, the club had his initiation performance on film. If he tried to quit, those pictures went to a good many places.

He shuddered again, imagining the reaction of his parents to the picture Betty had shown him. His parents were good people, but to say that they would not understand was like saying that lead would not float in water. They would never even go so far as to begin to understand.

Not in a million years.

And, he admitted, he could hardly blame them. What he had done, what he had participated in, defied understanding. It was all so incredibly wrong, so evil.

But he had done it. And now, when he wanted to stop doing it, his hands were neatly tied. The evidence of past sins forced him to resume his sinning. He felt like a criminal attempting to go straight, with his racket buddies threatening to expose him unless he continues to steal.

It was terrifying.

He poured the rest of the beer into his glass and worked on it. That, he knew, wasn't all there was to it. The worst part of all was his own miserable reaction to what he had been forced to do. Kissing Betty in that way had been horrible, revolting.

But he had been neither horrified nor revolted. He had been stimulated, excited beyond control.

And this was bad.

Because now he didn't know what to do. Maybe he could do what Betty had done—submerge himself in Libertine activities until the poison that ran through the organization and that was beginning to flow in his bloodstream multiplied a hundredfold and dominated him entirely.

Maybe that was the best way.

But could it be? He had managed to find a woman, a girl he needed.

Jan.

At first he had wanted both Jan and the Libertines. Now he knew that such an arrangement was absurd. He would only succeed in corrupting the girl, or else he would alienate her entirely. Now, for the time being, he was two people—Dave Forrester the Libertine and Dave Forrester the nice guy. But, if he went on playing the libertine, the nice-guy role had to disappear. It was inevitable.

He couldn't have his cake and eat it too. Or, in another sense, he couldn't eat his Betty and have Jan too. It would never work out that way.

He finished the beer.

"Another?"

He looked up at the barmaid. She was holding her shoulders back, purposely accentuating the thrust of her breasts against the front of her apron. Her smile was different now, he noticed. Obviously, she wanted to be had, and by him. But the smile was more than blatantly sexual. It was friendly as well, and he got the definite impression that, although she wanted to, she didn't want to with just anybody.

She wanted him.

"Sure," he said. "Another beer."

She brought him the beer. Then she took his glass and poured the beer for him, leaning forward as she did so. He looked down the front of her dress and saw that she was not wearing a bra. Her breasts were large and creamy.

Her eyes darted to either side. Then they returned to him, apparently satisfied that no one was seated within hearing distance of a whisper.

"I get off at three," she said.

"I thought the bars close at four."

"This one closes at three. You want to pick me up then, I'll wait for you."

He didn't know what to say.

"We could go have coffee," she said. "Or up to my place. I'll make some coffee and we can sit around and talk. I got a place of my own. No family. It gets lonely."

What was he supposed to tell her? That he had just had a

woman and would be out of shape for the rest of the night? If there was one thing he didn't want now, it was an argument. Better to tell her he'd be back and then to stand her up.

"I'll come back at three," he told her.

"I'll wait for you."

He sipped his beer.

"My name's Marge," she said.

"Dave."

"College student?"

He nodded.

"I went to City for a year. Then the old man died and I had to work or starve. So I've been here for two years."

That surprised him. She was only a year or so older than he was. She looked older—maybe because she had been on her own more. That could do it.

They talked aimlessly for a few more minutes. Then she drifted off to take care of another customer and he decided it was time to go, almost twelve-thirty. He raised the glass of beer to his lips and drained it. There was a little beer left in the bottle and he poured it into the glass. Then he drank it down and stood up, ready to go.

She hurried to him. "Going already?"

"I have to. I'll be back for you."

"Sure," she said. "Hell, I wish you didn't have to go. You don't know how lonely it gets here. A girl can go out of her mind believe me."

He gestured around the bar. "There must be plenty of people to talk to."

She laughed bitterly. "Slobs," she said. "Drunks, the same ones every night. Pigs. Either they don't talk to you at all or they're always pinching your behind and saying dirty things. There's never anybody nice in this hole."

She probably liked it when they pinched her behind, he thought to himself.

"Well," he said, "I'll see you."

"Don't forget now."

"I won't," he assured her.

"Because I'll be lonely otherwise. I make a damn good cup of coffee, Dave."

"Three o'clock," he said. "On the button."

He walked out of the bar and into the night. It was still raining, a little harder than before, and this time he noticed it. He headed north on Broadway, bucking the rain and the wind that was whipping it along.

And he tried to forget how alarmingly nice her breasts had looked when she had leaned toward him.

The bum brushed into him. "Mac," he whined, "I need a drink. I wouldn't ask you for a dime for coffee. Everybody asks for a dime for coffee. They don't want coffee. Any bum says he wants coffee is lying like a rug. Tell the truth, coffee'd kill me. Kill me dead. What alky does to your system, it makes it so you can't eat anything else. I need wine. So I won't ask for ten cents for a cup of coffee. How about fifteen cents for a glass of wine?"

He stared at the bum. It was easily the longest speech any bum had ever made to him, and he almost abandoned his policy of chasing bums away without a second thought.

Almost.

But not quite.

"Go away," he told the bum.

"It's a case of helping your fellow men," the bum said quite reasonably. "You're a student. Students should develop solidarity with bums. Hell, I was in the IWW. The wobblies. I could sing Joe Hill's songs to you if I wanted. So why don't you come up with fifteen cents for a glass of wine?"

"Go to hell."

"Fifteen cents," said the bum, unhappily. "Or a dime. Or a nickel. Anything."

"Go chase yourself."

"How about a cigarette," the bum suggested. "One cigarette, to chase the blues. Huh?"

He shouldered the bum away and walked on swiftly. He found a coffee joint that was open. The waitress was over fifty and homely as sin. She didn't smile at him or at anyone else. He ordered a cup of coffee and waited for it to cool.

He thought about the barmaid.

He didn't want her, not in one sense. He didn't want her, just as he didn't want the Libertines, just as he didn't want Betty Stacey.

But he liked her. His first impression of her was one that was changing slightly. At first he had thought of her as a slut, pure and simple, a wanton who saw a man, warmed up, and got ready for bed. It wasn't that simple. Basically, he decided, she was a nice kid. She wasn't a virgin, admittedly and obviously, but virgins were a very rare commodity to begin with and a drug on the market anyway.

She had seen him, and she had decided that she was lonely and that he was nice. She wanted him to spend some time with her. The way she saw it, her body was a trading point. If he could sleep with her, then he would be willing to be with her.

Or, he thought, it might work a little differently. More likely she wanted him to spend some time with her, and accepted sexual companionship as a natural accompaniment to any other type of companionship. Looked at in that light, the girl ceased to be a tramp at all.

And who was he to make moral judgments?

No one at all.

He stirred the coffee, then took a sip. It was strong and black and not too bitter.

What now? He shrugged, thinking that he really didn't have any choice in the matter. He would stay with the Libertines, because there was no way in the world for him to avoid staying with the Libertines.

He was stuck.

And Jan? Well, Jan was a lost cause, pretty much. But he would let things go along in much the same way that they had been going along. He would see Jan the regular two times a week, and he would let the sex bit start building up, and eventually he would get Jan, deflower her properly, and break her to harness. Then, perhaps, he would get Jan to join the Libertines the following year. That would be nice.

It would be great, he thought sourly. He hadn't been serious when the thought came to mind, but he took the mere thought that had occurred to him as strong evidence of how rapidly he was sinking into depravity. It was one thing to seduce a girl like

Jan, and quite another to contemplate making a perverted little whore out of her. And yet the thought had come to mind, seriously or not.

He wondered if he would do just that.

Maybe he should cut his ties with her now while there was still time. If he became a pure and simple Libertine, he could last the three years until his days at the college were over and done with. He could even enjoy himself. Each year there would be a new pair of girls to bed down with. Each week there would be a new book to read at the club, a new movie to watch, a new perversion to experience.

Maybe that was the answer. That way he could enjoy himself. But could he stand himself? Could he possibly stomach the person he would inevitably become?

That was another question.

Another question entirely.

And he knew the answer.

The answer was *No!*

He sipped his coffee, finished it, waved at the waitress and ordered another cup. He got a pair of hamburgers to go with the coffee. They weren't bad and he was very hungry all of a sudden. He wolfed the burgers down and drank more coffee.

No chance with Jan.

No chance with the Libertines.

No chance at all.

It was ridiculous, he told himself. He was a hot nineteen years old, and already he was trying to get around to admitting to himself that his life was a waste of time. At this rate it wouldn't be long before he went to the bathtub and opened his veins in it.

That would be a brilliant maneuver. But, when you came right down to it, what the hell else was he going to do? Just how was he supposed to go on living?

It was quite a problem. Too much of a problem, in fact, and he decided not to think about it. What he needed was something to take his mind off his problem.

Which was easy enough to find.

He called the waitress over. She added up his check and he paid her, leaving a tip because both service and food had been adequate.

Then he walked out again. He headed back down Broadway, headed for the bar where Marge worked.

She was waiting for him.

CHAPTER 9

"I didn't think you were coming."

"I told you I would." He grinned, then helped her on with her raincoat. *I didn't think I was coming myself*, he thought. *How about that?*

"I know you did," Marge said. "It was the way you said it. I had a feeling."

"Well, I came."

"And I'm glad. We can walk to my place. It's just around the corner. That's one of the advantages of this damn job. I live close to it. No long walk home at night."

He took her arm. "It must be quite a job."

"Twelve hours a day," she said. "Start at three and quit at three. Seven days a week."

"God!"

"It's easy work," she said. "Most of the time I just sit and let the television set talk to me. I'm only working now and then. Another guy takes care of cleaning up and everything. All I do is tend the bar."

"It must be something," he said. "I mean, all alone in a bar working those hours. You must get a lot of guys who try to make passes. Fresh guys."

She shrugged. "A few. Mostly neighborhood trade, the same

ones every damn night. But a few fresh guys. You get that any-
where you go."

"What do you do?"

"I hit them."

He looked at her, dubious, and she laughed.

"Not with my hands, for Christ's sake. There's a billy behind
the bar. Heavy wood. Hickory, I think. You swat a guy with that
and he stops making trouble. A cop I know had a club he wanted to give me—wood on the outside and lead on the inside. I
wouldn't take it. I figured I didn't want to kill some poor slob just
because he couldn't keep his hands to himself. And a club like
that would go right through a guy's head without stopping to say
hello. Not for me, Dave."

She stopped, tugging at his arm. "Here we are," she said. "I'm
on the third floor and it's a long way up. Take a deep breath and
let's go."

The building was an old brownstone, fairly rundown. They
walked together to the third floor. She had a front apartment and
opened her door with a key.

"Come on in," she said.

He followed her into the apartment. It was cheaply but deco-
ratively and tastefully furnished, and he was certain at once that
she had rented it unfurnished and bought the furniture herself.
A few pictures hung on the walls, prints of Post-impressionist
and Surrealist stuff, and he was surprised for a moment that she
liked that type of work. He had thought of her as an uneducated
tramp. Now he remembered the year at college and was ashamed
of himself for being a snob. Just because she worked for a living

he had automatically assumed that she was a moron. It was a bad way to think.

"It's not the greatest place going," she said. "But it's big enough to suit me. I can't stand living cramped. There's this living room plus a little bedroom and a separate kitchen. And a john with tub and shower. As soon as I get the money saved up I'll replace that couch before it falls apart completely. In the meanwhile you can sit on it while I get the coffee going. I'll only take me a minute or so."

"None for me, thanks."

"No coffee?"

"I've been sitting in a coffee pot for an hour or more," he said. "I practically have the shakes from it already."

"Could you stand bourbon?"

"That's an idea."

"I've got a bottle somewhere," she said. "If I can find it we can forget about the coffee."

The bottle turned out to be Jack Daniels. She poured it over ice cubes and sat down next to him, handing him a glass. They touched glasses and drank.

The bourbon went down very smoothly. So did the second glass of it, and by then he was very loose inside, very relaxed, very calm.

So was she.

He put his arm around. her, letting his hand rest very gently on her shoulder.

She cuddled closer to him.

He smelled her hair. It smelled very clean and sweet. He wanted to bury his face in it, to drown himself forever in the sweet smell of her. He decided that he was drunk, and then he decided that he wasn't really drunk, and finally he decided that it didn't make a hell of a lot of difference. He was with her, and he was happy to be with her, and now he did not have to think about all the things that he didn't want to think about.

He was going to sleep with her, and he knew that it was a good thing. He couldn't possibly sleep alone, not the way he felt. It wasn't the sex part that was important. It was the idea of having someone next to him, of not being alone in an empty bed. The sex would be good, too—he was sure of it. But sex was secondary. Closeness, company—those things mattered a good deal more. They made all the difference.

"Dave, what are you thinking about?"

"I don't know. Nothing. You, maybe."

"You like me, don't you? As a person, I mean."

"Yes."

"I'm glad," she said. "I was worried. I don't make a habit of picking guys up at the place. I'm not trying to say I'm a virgin or anything like that. I'm not. Far from it. But I don't want you to get the idea that I'm a tramp ready to put out for anybody who happens to come along. I talk that way,I know. That's what happens when you spend all your time behind a bar. Your language goes to hell. But I can talk it without being it, if I'm making sense. I'm not a tramp."

"I know."

"I acted like one tonight," she said. "Picking you up like that. But you looked . . . I don't know. Lost, maybe. Very sad and very lonely. And I wanted to get a chance to know you. Otherwise you would have walked out of that bar and never come back. I didn't want that to happen."

"I glad it turned out the way it did."

"So am I."

They finished their drinks. "Dave—"

He looked at her.

"Please kiss me, Dave."

He kissed her. Her lips were very warm, very soft. He put his hands on her cheeks and kissed her again.

"That's nice," she said. "That's very nice. Now I'm not going to talk any more. I'm not going to say a thing. Be good to me, Dave. Be gentle with me."

He kissed her again. It was, strangely enough, a very different kind of kiss from those he had experienced.

It was a very honest type of kiss. Neither of them had to impress the other, to try to excite or seduce the other. It was a foregone conclusion that they were going to make love, but there was more to the kiss than that.

For one thing, it lacked the falseness of the too-passionate, super sexual kisses exchanged with girls in the Libertines. It was gentle, almost tender. His tongue slipped between her lips, touching her teeth, stroking her lips on the inside. Her mouth opened and the tongue went inside, touching, probing, darting. But the tongue was in no hurry. There was a time for everything. There was no need to rush, no need to stimulate.

She was wearing a blouse and a skirt. The blouse buttoned down the back. It fitted loosely around the neck, which explained why he had been able to see her breasts when she had shown them to him at the bar.

He unbuttoned the blouse. He did not hurry with it but took his time, opening each button in turn. He rubbed her back, stroking the solid smoothness of her skin. She had a good, broad back. She was a solid girl.

She sat very still while he slipped the blouse over her shoulders and removed it.

They sat there looking at each other. She was bare to the waist and very lovely. He saw her breasts not as breasts but as parts of her. The whole picture of her, the skirt, the bare chest, the shoulders lightly tanned from the sun (and he wondered how in the world she got a tan working every afternoon, and decided that she must have a sunlamp somewhere in the apartment) the throat and the face and the light hair.

He remembered in the bar how he had thought that she was not a pretty girl. He had been right—she was not pretty. *Pretty* demanded a quality which she simply did not have. It meant a facile neatness of features, a grace which Marge did not possess. But what she had was more important.

She had beauty.

He looked now at her breasts. They were very large but completely firm with no sag to them, no droop. The nipples were large and quite pink. The breasts themselves were very white. Evidently she kept them covered when she lay beneath the sunlamp. He was glad. He preferred them as they were.

He touched one breast, cupping it very gently in one hand. The flesh was very warm, and he could feel something communicate itself from her warm breast up through his arm to his brain.

Warm.

Soft.

Firm.

He cupped her other breast, then drew her to him. He put his arms around her and kissed her again. He was wearing a thin shirt and he could feel her bare breasts through it. The feeling was delicious and he wanted to intensify it.

He released her for a moment and unbuttoned his own shirt. He took it off, then took hold of her again. Her breasts were against his chest now.

And he was kissing her.

His tongue buried itself once more in her mouth. He kissed her, and he could feel her nipples beginning to stiffen with desire. They pushed insistently against his chest, and he kissed her more fervently, more passionately.

He released her.

"The bedroom," he said.

She pointed through a doorway. He stood up and she stood up a second later.

They walked through the doorway.

She had a bed and a dresser and a tiny nightstand. He closed the door and turned to her, his arms reaching for her. With a little cry, she threw herself into his arms, nuzzling her face against his chest. He stroked her back, her neck, and she was the only thing in the world that mattered.

They sat down on the bed.

Then she stretched out on her back, still wearing the skirt, still wearing nothing above it. Even in that position her breasts stood proud and full.

He lowered his head and began to kiss them.

His tongue raced over silken flesh like a hungry puppy. She

moaned softly, making little animal sounds that came from deep within her throat.

He took off her skirt.

And her panties.

He, too, was ready.

He went to her and he saw her looking at him without embarrassment. He thought suddenly that it would be impossible for either of them to be embarrassed with the other. He didn't know why but he knew it was so.

Now he lay down next to her, on his side, and she rolled over into his arms. He felt the clean sweet warmth of her from her legs to her breasts, and he dropped one hand behind her and pressed her buttocks, drawing her in to him.

Then he rolled her over onto her back again. He crouched over her, and her warm solid thighs made room for him.

It began.

Slowly, at first. Their bodies knew each other instinctively, but they warmed up to one another slowly, gently. He did not want to hurry anything. He wanted to be as gentle with her as he knew how, as gentle as he possibly could. He knew that this was good, better than good, more than good, and he wanted to do nothing to spoil it.

Her hands stroked his back.

Her lips probed his mouth.

Her breasts were warm cushions for his body, soft sweet pillows of warm flesh.

He buried himself deep within the secretness of her warm body, feeling nothing in the world but the sweetness of her, tasting nothing but her mouth and feeling nothing but her.

Then, gradually, faster.

Much faster.

She was breathing heavily now, and he noted without much surprise that his breathing was precisely in time with hers. He was glad of it.

He was struggling to climb to the summit of the tallest mountain in the world. The way was steep and rocky, but no force on earth could prevent him from reaching his goal. She was with him, and they were climbing together, helping each other. Every step brought them closer to the very peak of the most majestic mountain in the world.

It was a height no human had ever reached before.

Higher and higher they climbed. He could not breathe, could not think. He could only respond to the wonder of her body, could only take his pleasure with her and give her a world full of pleasure in return.

Higher . . .

The world dipped and soared. They were almost there, inches away, and his brain began to burn with a fever that was rich and full and sweet. The springs of her bed groaned in mechanical pain and the walls seemed to shake with the very enormity of what they were doing.

Higher—

The day turned to night, the night to day. The sun went out and the moon turned black.

Higher!

And then they stood together at the high point of the world, the top of the universe. The world trembled beneath them and rocked from the force of their love.

The peak.

Perfection.

Then at once the mountain groaned and crumbled beneath them. It fell away, a heap of dead dust, leaving them suspended forever in the middle of the air.

"It's never been like that," she said.

He couldn't say anything.

"You don't know," she said. "You don't know how much I needed this. It was different for me than for you. It happened for me the minute you walked through the door. I saw you and I knew it was going to be like this. It's been so long, Dave. Months, maybe longer. I've needed a man so much I could taste it, and then you walked in, and I knew that you were the man I needed. I didn't have to know anything about you. All I had to do was see you. Is that ridiculous? I don't care. I don't care about anything. Tonight was heaven. That's all."

He kissed her.

"I think I'd like a cigarette," she said. "A cigarette would go good right about now. Would you like a cigarette, Dave?"

"Sounds good."

"I think there's a pack on the night table. Can you reach them?"

He found cigarettes and matches. He gave her a cigarette, took one for himself and lit them. They lay there smoking in silence for a few minutes.

"It's dangerous to smoke in bed," she said. "But I don't care. I read a book once where a woman said the main point of sex is so you can really enjoy a cigarette. I wouldn't go that far, would you? It sounds a little extreme to me."

"For what we just did, you don't need a reason. It's its own reason."

"It was good, wasn't it?"

"Perfect."

She sighed.

"Something wrong?"

"Nothing."

"What's the matter, Marge?"

"I don't know."

"Something on your mind?"

"Not really."

He stubbed out his cigarette in an ashtray, rolled over and touched her breast. He squeezed her, then let his hand run down over her softly rounded golden bowl of a stomach to her thighs. He touched her very tenderly.

"Tell me about it, Marge."

She looked away. "You'll be gone in the morning," she said, quietly. "That's all. I don't want to make a fuss or anything. It's just that you'll be gone in the morning, and I'll miss you. That's all there is."

"How do you know I'll be gone?"

"Because nothing ever works out."

"I'll still be here, Marge."

"Maybe that's even worse," she said. "I'd get used to having you around. And nothing like that could ever work, Dave. I'm a barmaid and you're a college kid and never the twain shall meet. It won't work out."

"How do you know?"

"It never does."

"We never met before."

"Dave—"

"Let's not talk about it, Marge."

"All right."

The cigarette had burned down between her fingers and he took it from her before she burned herself. He stubbed it out. She said she had to go to the bathroom and he waited for her.

And he thought about what she had said, trying to decide whether or not she was right. He hoped she was wrong, but her words made sense. Even without the twin problems of the Libertines and the Jan bit, it would be tough enough for a couple like him and Marge to survive. A college boy was supposed to go with a college girl. Any other arrangement was asking for trouble. A shack-up was fine, but he and Marge couldn't be a shack-up as such. There would, inevitably, be a strong emotional attachment.

So what the hell was going to happen with them?

Good question.

Hell of a good question.

She came back and he looked at the easy grace of her as she walked.

She came to him, soft and warm, and lay down beside him. He was very tired, more than tired, emotionally and mentally and physically, and he put his face between her breasts and inhaled the overpowering fragrance of her.

And slept.

•   •   •

He woke up in an empty bed. He looked around, wondering what had happened to her. Then, suddenly, she appeared.

"Breakfast is served, milord. Would milord come into the living room?"

She curtseyed prettily. The effect was a weird one because she was still very naked. She was the type of girl who could walk around an apartment stark naked and get away with it.

He followed her into the living room, his eyes on her every step of the way, and he sat down at a card table that she had set up in the middle of the floor. A plateful of scrambled eggs with bacon sat before him, and he remembered sadly that he didn't like eggs. He took a bite anyhow and found out that they were delicious.

"I scramble them with a hunk of cheddar cheese," she explained. "It makes them taste better that way."

"None for you?"

"I ate a while back. You're a lazy guy, you know. It's almost one in the afternoon."

That meant another day's classes were shot to hell, but somehow he couldn't have cared less. He was sitting, quite naked, in a girl's apartment, and the girl was sitting, also quite naked, directly across from him. Somehow this seemed much more significant to him than any of his classes. Even ecology.

He lifted a forkful of eggs to his mouth and it disappeared. She filled his cup with coffee, then sat down again. The coffee was delicious.

He helped her with the dishes, then quite forcibly led her into the bedroom.

"I have to get to work," she said.

He reached around her from behind and held her breasts. He felt her knees weaken and knew that she was not going to put up much of a fight.

"It's one o'clock," he said. "And you don't have to be to work until three. So don't give me any of this nonsense. I know better."

She giggled. "You're too smart for me."

"Uh-huh."

"And I bet I know what you want to do."

"You think so?"

"Uh-huh."

"What?"

She giggled again. Then she squirmed in his arms, turning around and kissing him. Her arms went around him and she kissed him so passionately that he almost fell over.

"How's that for a starter?"

"Not bad," he admitted.

She reached for him, took him in her hand. "You're so pretty," she said. "I'd like to hold onto you like this and never let go of you. I'd just keep you like this forever. Do you like it when I hold you?"

"Can't you tell?"

Another giggle.

"But don't do it forever," he said. "Not forever. There are other things that have to be done."

"Like what?"

"I'll show you."

"Show me."

She giggled again and twisted away from him, giggling hysterically, and when he reached for her she dodged him.

"Show me," she said.

"Give me a chance."

"You have to make me, Dave."

"That's what I'm trying to do, idiot."

She started to laugh again. But this time his hand shot out and touched her and the giggle stopped when passion soared up and drowned it.

She was ready now.

He had thought that nothing could possibly equal the night before.

He was wrong.

This was different—lighthearted lovemaking, quick and passionate pleasure between a man and a woman who knew each other well.

But it was just as good. Every bit as good.

And, when finally he moaned and she moaned and they rolled free of one another, limp and tired and exhausted yet strangely refreshed, strangely restored, he knew something he had not known before.

He loved her.

CHAPTER 10

He knew just what he had to do.

First, of course, she left for work. She explained that she had a bar to tend, that she had to be there for the next twelve hours much as she would have preferred to stay in bed with him. He lay in bed while she took a fast shower, then watched her while she dressed.

It was a joy to watch her.

"I'm going now," she said.

"What do you do about dinner?"

"Close up for half an hour. Around six, usually. Come home and cook a quick meal. Why?"

"Have dinner with me."

"You sure?"

"Of course I'm sure. That's a pretty silly question, wouldn't you say?"

"Maybe. I'm a pretty silly girl."

"You're a pretty great girl."

"I'm glad you think so."

"I know so. Could I have a kiss?"

She kissed him.

"I'll drop by the bar around six," he said. "Then we can duck out for a bite."

"Why not let me cook?"

"Uh-huh. I'm buying you a dinner."

Her face darkened. "You don't have to, Dave. Last night and today were free. There's no charge. You don't have to spend money on me to feel that we're coming out even."

He stood up. "Say that again and I'll slap the living hell out of you."

"I'm sorry."

"You better go to work," he said. "Right now, before I drag you back to bed again. I'll see you about six. And don't talk the way you just did again or I'll be mad."

"I bet you're funny when you're mad."

"Go to work," he said. "Now."

When she left the apartment was strangely empty. He took a shower and dried off in a hurry. He got dressed and wished he had clean clothes to put on.

Then he went back to his dormitory. He had things to do and only a short amount of time to do them.

First he sat down to his typewriter, rolled a sheet of stationery into place, and wrote a relatively difficult letter. He was glad, however, that he was not as close to his parents as some boys his age were. This made it easier.

He told them that he had decided to withdraw from the college. He explained why in a very vague sort of way, more or less hinting that he had a job offer which he did not want to turn down. He did not feel compelled to explain himself very carefully. His obligation, as far as he was concerned, consisted of telling them he was leaving and letting them know that everything was all right. That was the most important thing.

So he left out the details.

The next letter was to the school. It was short and to the point. He gave formal notice of his withdrawal from the college and instructed the school to send any tuition and dormitory fee refund that he had coming to his parents. This was an easy letter to write. The school was a huge institution, and he did not even remember seeing the person to whom he addressed the letter. It was formal and businesslike, and that was that.

The next letter was to the Chief of Police.

It was a more complex letter. It suggested that the Chief might be interested in attending a meeting at nine o'clock Friday night at 190 Spring Street. For the Chief's convenience, he enclosed a list of persons likely to be at the meeting. He named them all—Keith Talbot and Avery King and Marty Pekorsky and Clark Reynolds and Jeff Cruikshank, Leila Morse and Sally Chen and Elaine Rice and Sandy Wilkins and Mary Stackpole and, of course, Betty Stacey.

He gave the Chief a very thorough report on the activities of the club. He made it straightforward and to the point, and he pulled no punches. He had no need to pull punches.

Then he put the letters in envelopes, stamped them, sealed them, and dropped them in a mailbox. He had decided against writing Jan a letter.

She would find out that he had left, and that would be that. He had nothing to say to her.

Because what could he say?

He could say that very suddenly any continuation of the courtship they had played at was out of the question, that he was no longer the kind of boy who could make her happy. But these things would only confuse her.

Better to simply leave.

He went back to his dormitory, trying to decide what things to pack and what to leave behind. The problem turned out to be an amazingly simple one. He filled one suitcase with some necessary clothing plus those few items that could be converted quickly into ready cash. He took his typewriter down to the college store, which maintained a market in typewriters, and sold it for thirty dollars. His records, his books, most of his clothes—these things would have to remain behind. He had no use for them.

None at all.

His roommate walked in just as he finished packing.

"Hey," said the roommate. "Guess you're moving out a hundred per cent, huh?"

Dave nodded.

"Must be quite a broad."

"Huh?"

"Don't kid me," Bill Jergens said. "You don't move out of your room unless it's to shack up with a broad. And the way you've been spending your nights out lately—I can put two and two together. She any good?"

"No broad," he said, tired.

"Aw—"

"I'm leaving school," he said.

"Huh?"

"Joining the army?"

"In the middle of the term?

"That's about it."

"You must be out of your head. Why don't you take a cold shower or something and then think about it?"

He didn't even feel like lying any more. He picked up his suitcase, noticing with pleasure that it was not heavy at all. He started for the door.

"Look," he said to Jergens. "I have a lot of books and records here, some clothes, junk like that. You take care of them, will you? Save me trouble."

"Man, you'll be gone two, three years!"

He sighed. "You dumb bastard," he said, "I'm not asking you to *hold* them for me, for Christ's sake. I'm giving them to you, stupid."

"You mean it?"

"Of course I mean it."

"Well, hell . . . thanks."

He walked out of the room and down the hall, leaving Bill Jergens to mull that one over. It was a victory for Bill Jergens any way you look at it. He got rid of a roommate he didn't especially care for, had the room as a single with twice the space, and inherited enough records and books to start a store with. Not only that, but he'd be a conversational wizard for awhile. The hall would talk about Dave Forrester for at least a week, and everyone would presume that Bill was an authority.

He left the dorm. Then, with his suitcase swinging from his hand, he walked jauntily down Broadway to 95th Street. The sun was shining and it was a beautiful day.

    •   •   •

She smiled when she saw the suitcase. "Well, what do you know," she said. "You're moving in. I don't remember inviting you, but I guess I'll have to put up with you."

"Close up," he said.

"I usually wait until six. It's only ten to. Why not have a beer and relax?"

"Close up," he said. "Now."

She started to say something, then changed her mind. Quickly she shooed the few remaining customers out of the bar. Then she came out from behind the bar and joined him.

"What's up?"

"Let's go find a restaurant."

She tossed her apron on the counter and they went out to find a restaurant. He carefully avoided saying anything until they were halfway through with dinner.

Then he hit her with it.

"We're leaving town," he said. "Tonight. You're quitting your job and we're getting out of New York. I'm not sure where we're going. Cleveland, Chicago, Detroit—some place like that. I'll get a job there. You'll work, too—for a little while, anyhow."

She stared at him.

"You were right," he said. "It can't work out—me a college student, you a barmaid. It just won't work that way. But what we've got is too good to louse up. I don't want to chance losing it. You're too important to me."

That would do for the moment, he thought. Later, perhaps, he would tell her the whole story. But it was too involved for the time being. And what he had told her was the essence of the matter. She was the main reason. The rest was trimming.

"Tonight?"

"Tonight."

"I have money in the bank. I can't draw it out until morning."

"You can get it by mail."

"It has to be tonight?"

He nodded.

"I can't give notice at my job?"

"To hell with them. You're not even going back there this evening. No reason why you should have to."

She hesitated for only a second. "I'm not even going to ask what it's all about," she said. "I read the Bible once. Book of Ruth. The whither-thou-goest bit. I guess I understand what it means now. It makes sense."

He called the waiter, paid the check and left a tip. He took the suitcase with one hand and her arm with the other.

"Let's get to your place," he said. "And get you packed. One suitcase—no more."

"I'll have to leave a lot behind. But I've got you. I guess that's enough."

They hurried to her apartment and he felt there was a purpose for him now for the first time.

My Newsletter: I get out an email newsletter at unpredictable intervals, but rarely more often than every other week. I'll be happy to add you to the distribution list. A blank email to lawbloc@gmail.com with "newsletter" in the subject line will get you on the list, and a click of the "Unsubscribe" link will get you off it, should you ultimately decide you're happier without it.

Lawrence Block has been writing award-winning mystery and suspense fiction for half a century. You can read his thoughts about crime fiction and crime writers in *The Crime of Our Lives*, where this MWA Grand Master tells it straight. His most recent novels are *The Girl With the Deep Blue Eyes*; *The Burglar Who Counted the Spoons*, featuring Bernie Rhodenbarr; *Hit Me,* featuring Keller; and *A Drop of the Hard Stuff,* featuring Matthew Scudder, played by Liam Neeson in the film *A Walk Among the Tombstones.* Several of his other books have been filmed, although not terribly well. He's well known for his books for writers, including the classic *Telling Lies for Fun &f Profit,* and *The Liar's Bible.* In addition to prose works, he has written episodic television (*Tilt!*) and the Wong Kar-wai film, *My Blueberry Nights.* He is a modest and humble fellow, although you would never guess as much from this biographical note.

Email: lawbloc@gmail.com
Twitter: @LawrenceBlock
Facebook: lawrence.block
Website: lawrenceblock.com